BOY ON DEFENCE

BOY ON DEFENCE

Scott Young

M&S

An M&S Paperback from
McClelland & Stewart Inc.
The Canadian Publishers

An M&S Paperback from McClelland & Stewart Inc.

Copyright © 1953 Scott Young
Copyright © 1985 Scott Young

Reprinted 1993

Canadian Cataloguing in Publication Data

Young, Scott, 1918-
Boy on defence
ISBN 0-7710-9089-7
I. Title.
PS8547.095B692 1985   jC813'.54   C85-098445-9
PZ7.Y68Boy 1985

Cover design by Pronk & Associates
Cover illustration by Rob MacDougall

Printed and bound in Canada

McClelland & Stewart Inc.
The Canadian Publishers
481 University Avenue
Toronto, Ontario
M5G 2E9

Boy On Defence

CHAPTER 1 ◾

It was the night before the opening game of the high school hockey season. Bill Spunska had been in bed for an hour. He hadn't even started to feel sleepy. He twisted and turned and tried to will himself to sleep. He couldn't. In his ears was the roar of tomorrow night's crowd, the noise of skate-cuts on ice, the whacking of hockey sticks, the referee's shrill whistles, shouts from others on the Northwest team. His mind was like a movie screen and he was the big dark kid on defence, crouched and ready. The Kelvins were pounding in on him. He threw the check that broke up the big rush. . . .

Dreams. He grinned into the dark. It's easy enough to be a hero, in dreams.

He twisted again and tried to sleep, but in the creaking old house he could hear the wind under the eaves, the voices of his parents downstairs, the whisper of tires outside in the snow and slush of late November.

Another scene grew in his mind. It was the dressing room two days ago at the old rink where the school rented practice ice. The smell of sweat and liniment was heavy, as if years of those smells had soaked into the skate-scarred wooden floor and initial-carved walls. Rosy Duplessis, naked, wrung out his underwear until a small pool grew on the floor. Paul Brabant had the hiccups, as he almost always did in the letdown period after practice. Some of the boys sat still for a while before bending slowly to untie skate laces and get started on the business of undressing. Red Turner, the coach, was tearing a sheet of paper into small squares. Fat Abramson, the pint-sized student manager, was sharpening a stub of pencil with an old jackknife.

Then Red spoke. He had a gravelly voice. Last year it had taken Bill a while to get used to the fact that the hard voice and scarred face and burly shoulders once known well in the major league hockey rinks went with a man who was understanding and kind.

"I think we'd better elect a captain and alternates," Red said. "Last year Vic DeGruchy was captain. His alternates were Hurry Berton, Benny Wong and Junior Paterson. Paterson is gone."

"Why don't we just leave it that way?" Rosy asked.

"Well," Red said, "it's up to you guys. But we'll need one more alternate, anyway."

Vic DeGruchy's big red face came up from

his undressing. His frizzy reddish-blond hair stuck straight up. They all called him Grouchy, but he'd been a good captain, a tremendous leader on the ice. He said, "I nominate Spunska for the other alternate."

Pete Gordon said, "I second."

Bill started half off his seat. "I'm not even on the team for sure," he protested.

Red chuckled. "You're on! All in favour?"

Hands went up. Spunska, looking straight ahead, saw that there were many. Maybe all.

"Against?"

Nobody voted against.

"Spunska declared elected alternate," Red said. "And I made up those ballots all for nothing."

His last words were smothered in a warm hand clapping, and Bill sat there feeling – to his supreme surprise – tears close behind his eyes, a constriction in his chest, a desire to say something more than all he could say, which was, "Thanks."

He lay in bed now with his eyes open thinking of that amazing turn of events. *Alternate captain*. He still couldn't get over it. Last year he had been in only two games. He had pointed that out to Red Turner later, when they were the last two left in the dressing room. Red had said, "You underestimate yourself, kid. I've heard about some of the things you did in the off season to make yourself better. . . . That's the kind of stuff hockey players are made of."

Staring up into the dark, Bill wondered how much Red knew about what he had done to stay on skates after the hockey season was over last year. He'd thought nobody much knew, except maybe close friends, like Pete Gordon and Grouchy. A part-time job at the Arena had helped – manning the scrapers and shovels and brooms that augmented the ice-flooding machine for the Winnipeg Jets' late-season and playoff games. No pay, but it let him in free to see how NHL stars played the game. And until the ice thawed out of the corner-lot rinks in March, he'd been out every day. Sundays he'd do hundreds of backwards circuits, practising backward turns. And one day in summer, thinking of hockey, he'd experimented with a piece of wallboard and found that for shooting pucks its smooth surface was a lot like ice. Since September he'd been back at the Arena as a rink rat, for the Jets' camp and NHL exhibitions. Guess all that did some good. . . .

But this wasn't getting to sleep, darn it!

He concentrated on his room, item by item: the hooks in the corner, which held his clothes; the straight chair by the old bridge table, where he'd finished his homework two hours ago; the bookcase with its well-read books; the snapshot of Sarah Gordon stuck into the side of his bureau mirror; the two framed pictures of last year's Northwest team – one had been taken the night Pete Gordon's goal on Bill's pass beat Daniel Mac to win a place for Northwest in the playoffs, the other the night they lost out by one goal to Kelvin in the city Inter-High league final.

I'm glad it's Kelvin again tomorrow night, he thought. We'll beat them. We'll beat everybody. We'll win in the city and then in the province, we'll win everything we go after. . . .

Dreams again.

But he must have slept. Anyway, he didn't hear his parents come upstairs. When he came to consciousness again he could hear their voices in the bedroom next to his. The walls were thin. He couldn't help hearing.

The first word he heard was his father's "No!"

"Yes!" Mother said. "Andrew, I must go back to work." There was a pause and then her voice again. "I'm not going to have you working forever at those extra jobs at night to pay debts I caused."

Bill was wide awake now. Last winter she had been very sick. For weeks after a nervous breakdown she had lain in that room, the doctor saying that she should be in hospital but giving in to her pleading that she had been separated from her family too much already. Bill knew that her illness had scrambled the Spunskas financially. She had been working at a good job in the university's language lab. With two incomes they had been able to borrow $10,000 at the bank for the down payment on this house, carefully figuring (the two incomes again) that they could manage both the bank loan and the mortgage payments, as well as taxes and the usual expenses, heat, light, food, clothes.

It had seemed the turning point after years of tough times. Bill's dad, a professor in Warsaw, had been jailed for opposition to increasingly repressive laws to deal with the Solidarity movement headed by his friend Lech Walesa; and when released he had decided to leave Poland. He'd got Bill and Bill's mother out first, to England, but it had been more than two years before he could emigrate himself. Bill remembered the phone call that day in London when he'd heard the strained voice say, "Is Madame Spunska there?" and then, slowly, "Is that you, son?" He'd got permission for them all to go to Canada, where at first she'd worked as a maid and he had worked a year in pulpwood camps before being accepted as an assistant professor at the university. . . .

The voices rose again in the next room, Dad's voice, precise, accented English, half laughing, "I do not mind a little extra work!"

"I mind it for you! Teaching all day at the

university and again at night school! If you could spend that time on other studies . . ." Her voice softened now. "You need time to catch up."

"You think of me too much. It is enough that we are here together, our son with us, all of us happy. I would work twenty hours a day to preserve it. But I will not have you work and make danger for your health again. The doctor says you are not ready. You know that."

Then the voices were quiet. Bill lay with his eyes open. He had no thought of school or hockey now. In this family, his father's rule wasn't hard, but it was law. Bill knew that no matter how vehement his mother had been, she wouldn't try to go back to work now – and that left the money problem exactly where it had been.

Because he had been reminded, now he remembered an incident of a few weeks ago. It had been in the evening, downstairs, and he and Dad had been watching TV, Mother reading the paper.

She had said, "This chap who has been appointed associate professor in your department, how is he?"

"Good," Dad said.

"Are his languages as good as yours?"

"Not quite," Dad had said. "But he has been

here a little longer, knows more about this country. For teaching in Canada, his education is better balanced than mine."

No more had been said. But now Bill understood. Catch up . . . That's what they all had to do, each in a different way. When Bill had gone to Northwest first, the sports he was good in – cricket and soccer – were either not played at all, or played very little. The big sport was hockey, and he had decided he would learn the game. He smiled now in the dark to remember how bold that decision had been. He'd seen it at the first practice. He could hardly stand up on skates. The other boys, with a lifetime of Canadian winters behind them, skated as if their skates were as much a part of them as their legs, their arms, their eyes. So he'd catch up. The rink manager had given him a key and told him he'd be welcome to use the ice from six to eight every morning – there'd certainly be no one around to bother him! And then Pete Gordon had come down, and Vic DeGruchy, and morning after morning they had worked at the seemingly hopeless task of helping Bill Spunska catch up. Now Dad had to catch up, too.

But Dad was right. It couldn't be with the help of Mother working, and maybe breaking down again.

He closed his eyes and swallowed hard, in an excess of emotion he couldn't put down. When

Dad was in the North and Mother worked in a big home in the southern part of the city, Bill had been with her. The people had been kind. They had made quite a conversational point among their friends of the fact that their house-keeper was the wife of a Polish professor. Sometimes Bill had thought she didn't mind. But when they finally had financed the house and got off the bus at the end of the street a block from their new home, she had walked with Bill holding his arm tightly and with happy tears running down her cheeks. Nobody had guessed that the strain of years would soon catch up to her. But it had, and if the doctor said she wasn't ready to work again, it simply wouldn't happen.

Then the solution came to him. I'm the answer. I can work after school to help.

What about hockey? What about all those dreams? If I get a job, I'll have to give up a lot of skating time. And there are other things I'll lose, sport and conversation and friendship in hours that have been my own. I'm just starting to feel that I belong, a feeling I never had before. . . .

But it's a big chance to help, the first big chance of my life! It has to be done!

He turned his face into the pillow. Tomorrow I'll start looking. Wonder if I can find a job that'll leave time for practices and games? Maybe. Should I tell Mother and Dad? No. Not until I have a job. No use giving them anything more to worry about until it's all set. I'll do this on my own. . . .

The old house, full of the struggle of new hopes, groaned in endless restlessness.

Eventually mother, father and son slept quietly.

CHAPTER 2 ▬

When the noon bell rang through the wide bright halls of Northwest High the next day, most of the boys and girls streamed out of Room 41 immediately, some going home for lunch, others heading for the school cafeteria. Bill sat where he was, reaching into his desk for his brown paper bag of sandwiches. If he hurried he'd have time to slip across the street to the drugstore and buy a paper and look at the Help Wanted advertisements. Then he noticed that Sarah Gordon hadn't left with the others. They were alone in the room. She came toward him, smiling, and leaned on the desk across the aisle.

"Aren't you going home for lunch?" he asked.

"As soon as I put the bee on you."

They had been close friends for a year. She was slim and her hair was fair, eyes sort of gray. To Bill she was the prettiest girl in the room. She was also very direct. That's why he was a little uneasy now. You couldn't fool Sarah. Would what she was going to ask him affect his decision to look for a job – and also his decision not to tell anyone about it yet? "I hope it's something I can do," he said.

"It's easy."

"Fire away, then," he said.

"All you have to do is join the dramatic society."

"Dramatic society?" he asked, stalling.

"You knew one was being formed, Barrymore! The notices have been up for weeks. We had our first meeting last night. Only two boys turned up and twenty girls. I'm on the recruiting committee. And that brings us to you, sir, Mr. Spunska."

"I can't do it, Sarah," he said.

She didn't catch the seriousness of his manner. "Why not? You were in some plays in the school in England, so you have experience. We need it. None of the rest of us have. You and I might even wind up in the same play. . . ."

He should tell her he had to get a job. She would understand, then. But if he wasn't going to tell his parents, he couldn't tell anyone. Besides, darn it, he'd often thought that too much of their friendship up to now had been founded on sympathy. At first, at least part of her quick interest in him had been of the sort which she'd naturally give to anyone who had come through a rough time. Then there had been Mother's illness, during which Sarah and Pete had called often and done everything they could to help. Now if he told her he had to get a job, she would guess the reason immediately – that his family needed the money. And that was nobody's business but their own. When he had the job, that would be different. People would have to know, then. But there was a difference in having a job, and looking for one. He shoved his big hands in the pockets of his jeans and stood up. When she misunderstood his pause and urged him again, the battle he'd been fighting inside made his answer too abrupt.

"I just can't, that's all!" he said.

He saw her puzzled, rebuffed look, but his own disappointment kept him from reacting to it. This was sacrifice number one.

"But why not?" she asked.

"I can't tell you, right now!"

They looked at one another. She had a quick, volatile temper. "All right, then!" she said, and walked from the room.

For a few seconds he stood there, head down, his fists clenched in his pockets. When he finally could tell her, she'd understand. He knew that. But he thought of how good the Gordons had been to him, the summer weekends at their cottage, the feeling that he was always welcome in their home. Now the first time she asked him to do something, he'd had to turn her down. She had a right to be annoyed. But he had to go this alone, for now.

Trying to put it out of his mind, he walked through the empty room to a window. The sun shone in an all-blue sky and last night's snow was melting and dripping from the roof. A few rubber-booted lategoers were hurrying home. One group in particular – four boys – were talking at a great rate and making a pantomime of shooting and checking some imaginary adversary. A quick surge of excitement wiped away everything else. They'd be talking about the game tonight, hoping we can knock off Kelvin. And that's what I should be thinking about, too, instead of moping around like this.

The corridors were almost deserted as he hurried to the washroom. He checked his nails and stood before the mirror, pushing a comb through his thick dark hair. The comb was almost lost in his big hands. He was big all over, six feet tall and with broad shoulders and thighs which bulged his denims. His jaw was as strong as the rest of him. Only in his eyes did his age show, a mixture of resolution and uncertainty, boy's eyes.

Just as he finished and turned away, the washroom door banged open behind him. It was Pete Gordon, Sarah's brother, Bill's best friend and Northwest's star hockey centre. Pete, fair-haired, short, with the compact build and springy step of the small athlete, was in Grade

Twelve now, a year ahead of Bill and Sarah. But he and Bill were the same age, nearly eighteen, Sarah a year younger.

"Come on, speedball!" Pete said, holding the door open, waving one hand urgently. "What've you been doing? Time's a-wastin'!"

And Bill's thoughts suddenly were fully on hockey. He wouldn't have time now anyway to go and buy a paper.

"Lineups up yet?" he asked.

"No, but what are you worrying about? You're on, Red said."

"Just wondered who's going to be the fourth defenceman." Last year Bill had played his two games on defence with DeGruchy. This year Red had split them up. He'd paired Rosy Duplessis with Bill. Grouchy had been practising sometimes with Knobby Warren, the new boy, and sometimes with Gordon Jamieson, who'd been a regular last year.

"Do you care?" Pete asked.

"I'd like to see Gord on the team," Bill said. "Must be tough to be on one year and have to struggle to make it the next. But that Knobby is pretty good. Hits like a truck."

As they left the washroom, Pete was grinning.

"What's the joke?" Bill asked.

"I was just noticing the way you talk. When you came here last year you had that English accent. I used to think it was peculiar, a Polish name and an English accent. Now you're just as slangy as the rest of us Canadians."

"My dad is always checking me up on it. Natural, I guess, hanging around with you mugs all the time."

Pete gave him a body check, for that, as they shoved open the door of the cafeteria. It was as airy and modern as the rest of the school, a lot of tile and glass. Over in one corner, near the swinging doors that led to the kitchen, was the hockey team's table.

As Bill and Pete passed through among other tables, Bill to pick up milk to go with his sandwiches, Pete to buy a hot lunch, the hum of talk lessened and many called out as they passed. Mostly the boys.

"Ataboy, Spunska! Murder those bums tonight!"

"Hiya, Bill, Pete . . ."

"Get a goal for me tonight, Pete!"

"Get a dozen!"

From the near-unknown of last year Bill had become a somebody, and it felt good.

The boys at the hockey table looked up. Paul Brabant, dark, good-looking, the goalie, said, "Here come Damon and Pythias now."

"David and Goliath," said Pincher Martin, centre on the third line. He had a huge napkin tucked into the collar of his shirt. Pincher was a flashy dresser. Even when he was only eating a sandwich he took as much care of his clothes as if he were preparing for a heavy rainstorm.

Rosy Duplessis chimed in, as usual. Rosy had been christened Rosario, but with cheeks as round and red as a good apple, he'd been Rosy from the cradle on.

"Look, you, Spunska," Rosy said, "you are now a big man on the team, but that is no excuse for being late. Watch out there, boy! We will trade you to St. John's Tech for four test tubes and a Bunsen burner!" Rosy laughed heartily, as he always did at his own jokes. He had moved here from Quebec and naturally spoke French as well as English, although, as he once had remarked, that was no recommendation for his French.

Pete sat in the middle of the row beside Benny Wong. Bill pulled out a chair and sat at one end, beside Vic DeGruchy. Grouchy had finished his lunch and was drinking a pint of milk. He grunted at Bill's greeting. On game days, he spoke only on matters of great importance.

Bill called "Hello" to the boys who were new to the team this year. They sat at the other side of the table together. Scotty McIntosh, freckled and red-headed and shy, played on a line with Pincher Martin and Benny Wong. Beside him was Knobby Warren, the defence candidate, a tough short boy whom everybody liked. Down at the far end were three kids who came out to every workout but didn't seem to have any chance of making the team unless disaster struck some of the others. They were Grade Tenners, all slight boys, Ward, Somerset and Michaluk. Rosy already had nicknamed their line the Three Ghosts. And then there was big Cliff Armstrong, whose dark handsome face had a habitually sullen expression.

"Hello, Cliff," Bill said.

"Hi."

Bill started on his sandwiches, wondering what made Armstrong the kind of guy he was. He'd met Armstrong first, last year, the night they were beaten 3-2 by Kelvin in the league final. After the hard struggling disappointment of giving all and finding it not enough, he and Pete had come up into the rink lobby and were heading toward Mr. and Mrs. Gordon and Sarah, waiting near the coffee bar, when they saw Alec Mitchell, left winger on Northwest's second line. Mitch beckoned and they went over. With Mitch was Cliff Armstrong, whom he introduced, and two men.

Armstrong had introduced the men as his brothers, Ike and Cam.

The men were quite a bit older than Cliff, in their twenties or early thirties. Bill and Pete said "Hello," and were about to pass on when the brother named Ike said, "What you guys needed out there tonight was somebody who could score a goal. You'll have him next year."

At first Bill thought the man was kidding. He was smiling, but wasn't kidding.

"Yeah," the other brother, Cam, said. "Too bad you didn't have Cliff out there tonight. Would have made all the difference."

Mitch explained that he lived a few doors from Ike Armstrong, the oldest brother, and that Cliff this year was playing with Brandon Collegiate – the team Kelvin would meet in the provincial final.

"Next year Cliff's coming down to live with me," Ike said. "So he'll be going to Northwest."

As Bill and Pete went on to join the Gordons, Bill met Pete's raised eyebrows. "There's a guy with his family right behind him," Pete said. "But I guess it'll be all right if he's as good as they think he is."

Armstrong, it turned out, was just as good as his brothers seemed to think. Brandon lost 4–2 to Kelvin in the Manitoba final, but Cliff scored both Brandon goals. And, as advertised, he'd come this year to live with his brother and move into Grade Eleven at Northwest. But from the first practice, he'd displayed an attitude of cockiness and defiance which had riled the others. He'd been quite caustic with Fat because he'd asked for sweater number 9 – Pincher Martin's number – and had been given number 14, which had belonged last year to Henry Bell, right winger on Pete's line, who had been graduated last June. During the five subsequent practices, as Armstrong quickly made a place on right wing of a line with Pete and Stretch Buchanan, a coolness had grown up around him. He seemed to have appointed himself the leader of the new boys trying out for the team. Bill had tried to avoid sharing the antagonism most of the old hands on the team showed toward Armstrong, but it was difficult. On the ice, he was a whiz. Off the ice, when he did say anything, it was usually a cutting wisecrack better left unsaid. There was only one bright spot – he and Mitch seemed to get along all right. In fact, they were quite chummy. So maybe there was some hope. . . .

Then Bill noticed that Stretch Buchanan wasn't at the table, although he always ate at school.

"Where's Stretch?" he asked.

"Flu," Grouchy said.

Pete stopped short, his fork halfway to his mouth.

Benny Wong, grinning all over his round bland face, said, "Never mind, Pete. I saw the coach this morning. He says he'll move Rosy up from defence to your line."

Pete groaned. Everybody laughed except

Rosy, who protested, "Don't laugh or groan, you, Pete! I'll be the best man out there, as you know!"

"You'd better be," Grouchy said.

Rosy grumbled. "You are all most impolite."

Benny Wong said, "That puts both Jamieson and Warren on defence, anyway."

"Yeah!" Pincher Martin said. "What we lose on the forward line we win on defence."

Rosy picked up a bottle of milk and made a motion as if he were going to throw it. That stopped Pincher cold. Armstrong treated this friendly byplay as if it didn't exist.

By the time they were finished eating, it was nearly one. Bill went back to the room for his coat and went outside with the others for a breath of fresh air. Heading back for the classrooms a few minutes later, Pete said, "What are you doing after school? Like to come over and listen to some records for a while?"

Bill said, "Not tonight, Pete. I've got something to do."

That something turned out to be not what he had expected. Somehow, he'd had a picture of himself tramping doggedly from place to place looking for work. For years the papers had been full of how hard it was for young people to get jobs, the usual message being that a young man wanting a job had to be prepared for weeks of pounding the pavements. He expected that.

When the final bell rang he hurried downstairs to the bulletin board, glanced at tonight's lineup to confirm what Benny Wong had said that noon, then avoided everyone else and went across the street to the drugstore and bought a copy of the *Telegram*. He resolutely skipped the sports page and began to read advertisements.

YOUTH, 16–18, willing to learn multilith . . . Permanent.

YOUNG MAN to assist in packing china, five-day week.

BOY WITH BICYCLE . . .

BOY for light work in boardinghouse.

DELIVERY BOY . . .

JUNIOR CLERK . . .

All these advertisements were for people to work full time.

Then he saw it.

STRONG student to work after school and Saturdays. Apply John Desmond, Limited, 55 Viaduct Street.

He was standing right on Viaduct Street. The drugstore where he'd bought the paper was 586 Viaduct. Bill turned and walked quickly north, clutching the paper, and every once in a while broke into a run. It was so exactly what he wanted that he was sure someone else would beat him to it. He made the five blocks in five minutes, and in gold lettering against the green painted window of a long neat cement-block building was:

JOHN DESMOND, Limited
(WHOLESALE ONLY)

He went in. Two young women were working on telephones at desks which faced one another behind a wooden rail. A thin young man with glasses was staring intently at a computer screen as his fingers poked here and there at the keyboard. When Bill stopped at the counter this young man looked up and said, "Anything I can do for you?"

"I'm looking for a job," Bill said.

The young man turned and called through a doorway to an older man, sitting in a tiny glassed-in cubicle off the main office: "Mr. McClelland. Are you busy?"

The older man, big, with a pleasant face and a small mustache, beckoned to Bill. "Come on in," he said. "Sit down." He lighted a cigar and looked at Bill for a minute while he did so, then suddenly took the cigar from his mouth, blew out smoke, and said, "Well, can you work hard? We've had lots of kids try this job. None last long. This is a tough Joe-job in the warehouse, helping the warehousemen put up orders. A lot of lifting."

"I'm sure I can do it, sir," Bill said.

"How much money would you want?"

Bill swallowed. "Whatever you would pay me, sir."

"Well," Mr. McClelland said. "That's a change! You mean you don't want to know how long it will be before you'll have my job, and how our pension plan works, and how much free insurance you get? The job pays five dollars an hour, for two hours a day, five days a week, and eight hours on Saturday. Eighteen hours, ninety bucks. You could start tomorrow. How's that?"

"Wonderful, sir!" Bill said. Then he remembered hockey. He'd been going to try to find a job that wouldn't make him quit hockey. For one thing, he was sure his father wouldn't let him take one that would force that sacrifice – not great, perhaps, to an adult, but one his father understood. "There's one thing, sir," he said, hoping this wouldn't ruin it all.

"What's that?"

"I play hockey for Northwest High. We practise one afternoon a week, Wednesday, after four." He hesitated. "I want the job, but if I could keep on at hockey, too . . ."

The man thought a few seconds, then said, "Tomorrow's Saturday. Let's leave the hockey thing until tomorrow night. By that time we'll know how you fit in out there. If you're okay, I think we can spare you one night a week – if you can spare the ten bucks you won't get. Eighty instead of ninety, right?"

"Right!" Bill said, and walked home on air. A fortune! Mother came from the kitchen to meet him. Her eyes were brown and seemed very large in her oval, attractive face. As usual she gave him a hug and smile. He hesitated on the brink of telling about the job. No. He'd wait until Dad came home.

But when Dad came in he greeted his wife and son cheerfully, then headed straight for the sofa and a nap.

Bill, his mind full of the job (eighty dollars a week!) as well as hockey, paced restlessly through rooms sparsely furnished with comfortable second-hand furniture. Once as he passed the living room door he paused, seeing how thin his father was, how lined his face under his thick greying black hair, although he was just forty. But there was a happiness in that face, too, something Bill knew was more important than any of the other appearances. He went upstairs, washed, came down, tried to sit still. He wondered how Dad would react about the job. He'd just have to agree to this! He couldn't carry the whole load.

Finally Mother called, "Dinner, you two . . ."

To Bill's surprise, Dad rolled quickly from the sofa and was first to the table.

"Weren't you asleep?" Bill asked, laughing.

"My boy," Dad said, "it is a queer thing, but for many years I could be asleep in Warsaw and someone in Krakow would whisper the word 'dinner' and I would immediately be awake. Even now, where I am well fed, this word has the effect of a shock of electricity."

They all laughed. Bill held his mother's chair. Dad said, "I wish we could go to see you play tonight, Bill. Too bad I always work on Fridays. I'll be home in time to hear the last part of the game, though."

Dad taught night school Mondays, Wednesdays and Fridays. All Northwest's games were on Fridays.

"We'll just have to see one before the season is over, though," Dad said. "We'll do it somehow."

"I'll be so excited," Mother said. "I'm excited already."

Dad looked at Bill and smiled. "So is Bill. Every hockey night."

Bill looked down at his plate and then up at his father and then at his mother. "It's more than the game," he said.

They looked at him curiously.

"Today I got myself a job," he said. There was a sudden silence. They stared at him. He went on quickly, telling them it wouldn't interfere with hockey. "And eighty dollars a week!" Still, as he spoke, he intercepted a stricken look between them, each asking the other, with that look, if he could have heard them last night.

"I heard," he said. "I couldn't help listening. This job will not be hard." He turned to his father and his words came with a rush. "I want to help! We can pay the bills together and then you can spend more time on the work you really want to do!"

His father thought a minute, his face serious and brooding. Bill waited. It was almost possible to read his father's mind. He was thinking, Bill knew, what he often had told Bill, that the classes were only part of school – a part which led to relationships and activities that were almost as important as the school itself. But he couldn't have foreseen Mother's sickness, and now those monthly payments were a huge burden.

Finally he shrugged as if at something he had to accept. "As long as it won't interfere with hockey, which means so much to you, I have to agree. But I'd like to make one condition. . . ."

Bill waited.

"With your help we can get back faster to the place where my salary from the university will look after all our needs. Then you will stop working."

As Bill said, "All right," he noticed that there were tears in his mother's eyes, and he continued, impulsively, "I want to make a condition, too, though! It is that we both work at these extra jobs until everything is paid, and then when I quit my job you will quit the night school, too."

His father looked at Bill for a long second or two, as if seeing there some strength and awareness he hadn't noticed before. "I agree, son."

And after dinner the three of them sat on at the dining room table for a few minutes. Dad pulled a notebook from his pocket and began to figure aloud. This gave Bill a queer feeling. It was like being let into a partnership, as he heard for the first time the details.

"We're behind in payments at both the bank and the mortgage company," Dad said. "They've both been good about it but sometimes they have pressed me and I just keep telling them I'm doing the best I can and they know what I make and they go along. But with help from you, say fifty a week – a loan, son, to be paid back later – we could handle things, not get in any deeper. We'd still have no reserve for emergencies, but . . . ."

"But I'll be able to give you eighty," Bill broke in.

Dad shook his head. "You'll put in fifty. You can save the rest or spend it, as you wish. But it is yours. Now you'd better eat and get to your game."

Dad had a way of saying some things that allowed no argument, not even discussion. This was one of those times.

CHAPTER 3 ▬

Bill closed the inside door and the big wooden storm door and took two strides across the slightly sloping wooden veranda and ignored the three shallow steps in a jump to the walk. Snow was falling, muffling the noises of the trains in the yards two blocks away.

He turned up his coat collar and walked quickly to the bus stop. The evening chill, sharp in his nostrils, had frozen the afternoon slush. The new snow was white and clean along the tiny front yards of the street. He watched the flakes, big and soft and thick, in the headlights of passing cars as he waited for a bus that seemed to take forever to come. As it dawdled over the twenty blocks southwest through the city to the rink, Bill sat by a window and watched the city go by, the hurrying downtown crowds, lighted windows, pretty girls, the warmth of bus and street and store lights in the snow. The excitement of this game and the season to come – How'll we go? Can we win it all? –

made an almost unbearable growing tightness in his chest.

And the new job! He wondered if Sarah had said anything to Pete about that encounter at noon. Now that the job was accomplished fact he felt different about telling about it. He wanted to tell about it now. He'd tell Pete and Sarah together. . . .

The bus pulled away from the last stop before the rink. Bill was first to the step. The conductor called, "Polo Park! Winnipeg Arena!" and said to Bill in a lower voice, "I'd like to be getting off here myself."

Bill hopped down into the crowd that was streaming from other buses and parking lots toward the big brightly lighted front of the Arena.

As he hurried through the crowd, people called to him. Three girls in hats topped by long wavering feathers, and ribbons of Northwest's colours, red and white and blue, pinned to the lapels of their swinging fur coats, smiled at him rather shyly and said, "Hello, Bill." Surprised, he smiled and said "Hello" back. Three boys with fur collars and big mitts slapped his back. "Swamp 'em tonight, Spunska!" they ordered. And Spunska said they'd try. Boys and girls from other schools, noticing the attention he was getting, peered at him, trying to figure out who he was.

Close to the Arena the throng slowed. People in front watched newcomers anxiously, waiting for friends. Bill was at the end of the line edging toward the turnstiles when he caught sight of Pete Gordon a few places ahead of him.

"Hey, Pete!" he called. "Back here!"

Pete swung around and saw him. He left his place in the line and came back and fell in beside Bill.

"Are we late?" Bill asked.

"Don't think so," Pete said, glancing at his wrist watch. "No. It's only seven. We've got half an hour."

"The crowd seems big for half an hour before the game."

"All come to see Northwest's new alternate captain," Pete said.

Bill laughed. "Of course." As they moved on, he said, "You'd make a better alternate captain than me, you know."

Pete shook his head. "I always figure a captain or alternate should be a big guy. Then when he's arguing with a referee he can tower over the guy, scare him to death."

"I've never seen a scared referee yet," Bill said.

"You'll scare 'em, kid," Pete said.

As they neared the gate, Bill wondered with a thrill part excitement and part apprehension how he'd make out the first time he had to argue a decision with a referee – a privilege allowed only to a captain or alternate. He and Pete talked about their own game with Kelvin, and about the second game of the double-header – St. John's Tech and Daniel McIntyre Collegiate. There'd been talk in the summer that some of the other city schools might institute hockey programs but it hadn't happened. Gordon Bell, the only other team in the Inter-High league, had a bye tonight but would play next Friday. The Inter-High had its own way of doing things: each team played four games before the Christmas break and four games after, then the playoffs. Not much compared to the long seasons played by juniors and professionals, but somebody, sometime, had had the bright idea that high school athletes shouldn't be playing so much that they couldn't keep up with their school work.

Suddenly Pete said, "Hey! You didn't hear the latest about Armstrong?"

"What?"

"The brothers," Pete said. "Fat came all the way over to my place after school to tell me. One of them phoned the coach at school today and suggested that Armstrong would look good at centre with the Chief and Stretch on the wings. Breaking up two lines, yet! He didn't tell Red what he was to do with the three centres from last year, either."

"What did Mr. Turner say to that?" Bill asked, half grinning. It was funny, in a serious sort of way. To separate Pete and Stretch Buchanan would break up a combination that had scored a lot of goals. And the Chief – Horatio Big Canoe, the Indian boy on the team – wouldn't want to leave the line he'd played on last year, either. Those brothers sure had a lot of crust.

"Told them he'd make his own decisions." Pete sighed. "I've got an idea that Armstrong's brothers are about three-quarters of his trouble. If they'll do *that* – phone up the coach and tell him how to run the team – they're probably yapping at Cliff all the time, too, telling him he's getting a raw deal, all that stuff. It's the only thing I can figure out to explain why he acts the way he does. Nobody on the team has ever done him dirt, that I know of. You heard of anything?"

Bill shook his head. He wished that Fat hadn't told about that phone call. If people started ribbing Armstrong about that, no telling what would happen. But Bill was still too full of his job to think about Armstrong indefinitely. He wished Sarah was with Pete. Then he could have told them both at once about his job and explained why he couldn't tell her at noon.

"Your parents here?" he asked Pete.

Pete nodded. "Back there somewhere, with

Sarah." He glanced obliquely at Bill and smiled. Bill returned the smile. Sarah couldn't have said anything, or Pete wouldn't be carrying on this usual mild teasing.

He showed his player pass to the doorman and shoved through behind Pete and then they were almost out of the crowd, for the others admitted through the turnstile were rushing across the wide lobby toward the corridors leading to their seats. As Pete and Bill passed the lobby coffee bar Lee Vincent, the sports columnist for the *Telegram*, was there, talking to another man. Lee Vincent was a small sandy-haired man in his early thirties, who limped slightly from an attack of polio he'd suffered in his teens. The other man, older, was short and chubby, with a small mustache and a merry expression.

The sportswriter saw them and waved. They called "hellos" as they went by, and on the stairs Pete said, "Well, well!"

"What?"

"Know who that was with Lee Vincent?"

"No."

"Squib Jackson, the head scout for the Toronto Maple Leafs!"

Bill stopped short at the bend of the stairs and looked back, and saw that the scout and the sportswriter were looking after them as they walked. As he followed Pete after that brief backward look, he wondered what they'd be saying. He knew enough of the workings of the National Hockey League teams to know that the presence of scouts here wasn't unusual. Their main interest would be the junior amateur teams, from which players were drafted once a year by the twenty-one teams of the National Hockey League. Only rarely a player was good enough to make pro in one jump from high school, but Barker, Kelvin's star defenceman last year, was playing for Boston's farm team in the East right now. Bill wondered who the Toronto scout was interested in here tonight.

Lee Vincent was a modest man, and gave his opinions without being emphatic. He liked Squib Jackson and he knew that the scout liked him. In the past Jackson often had asked his advice on players being scouted by Toronto. As Pete and Bill passed, Lee said, "Northwesters. The little guy is Pete Gordon."

"I've seen him," Squib said. "He's a pretty hot centre. Who's that big kid?"

"Bill Spunska. A defenceman."

The scout looked as if he were trying to remember something. He brightened suddenly. "Is he the kid you wrote the story about last year? The kid who was going down to the rink every morning to learn how to skate?"

Lee nodded.

Downstairs Bill and Pete ran into Rod McElroy, the spare goalie. He was a husky boy, his hair very blond. His mother was dead, his father an air force officer who had been moved to Winnipeg a few months ago.

"Lucky guy," Pete said, "sitting this one out while we slave over a hot puck."

McElroy grinned. "Don't kid about a serious thing like that. I'd like to stay in one city long enough just once to do somebody out of a goal-keeping job. Probably won't be this year, though. Dad was telling me just last night he might get another sudden move any time. . . . And when the air force says sudden, they mean sudden."

"Hope it isn't before the end of the season," Bill said.

"So do I."

As they were talking, they passed Red Turner in the corridor. He was heading upstairs on some business or other. The dressing room was about half full when they arrived. One player was fully dressed – Scotty McIntosh, the new winger on Pincher Martin's line.

"Sure you'll be ready in time, Scotty?" Pete joshed him, and the boy flushed as he smiled.

A chorus of "Hi" and "Hello" went around the room, with some kidding back and forth, and Bill and Pete looked for their uniforms among the small stacks laid out neatly at intervals on the bench around the wall.

"Down here, you mugs!" It was the deep voice of Fat Abramson, the student manager. As usual, he was bustling around helping players on with the more complicated parts of their pads, lacing shoulder pads, supplying tape for players to tape their shin and knee pads into position, fussing like a Bantam hen.

Right now, he was helping Rosy Duplessis. Next to Rosy was a stack of pads with a sweater folded on top to show Bill's number 4. Next was Pete's number 15.

As they slipped quickly out of their clothes, Bill felt the excitement rising in him again until he could scarcely bear it, everybody talking and kidding, and the dressing room had the same feeling as last year, when this team was eager and untried and every game was an adventure. Then Alec Mitchell did a shuffle-off-to-Buffalo into the room and Armstrong came in behind him, grinning. Bill was just thinking that, with a little time, Armstrong would be all right, when the lightning struck.

"Well, well, well," Hurry Berton said. "If it isn't the all-star centre!"

Mitchell looked at Armstrong, then at himself, then behind them.

"Not you, Mitch," Berton said.

It was evident immediately that Armstrong knew what Berton was talking about. He caught looks from a few others in the room who also knew.

"I didn't have anything to do with that!" he said. But then he seemed to regret going back on his brothers, for when Berton started to talk again Armstrong told him abruptly to shut up.

The uninformed among the others were listening wide-eyed. "What the heck's that all about?" Rosy demanded.

Bill, with his back to Rosy, gave Fat a look which he hoped said, "Shut up!" Rosy would find out all right, so many knew. But give it time to cool, now. Fat got the look, all right.

Then the coach came in and the talk died down.

Bill was all dressed now – leg pads, shoulder pads, heavily padded pants – except for his sweater and skates. He sat for a few seconds sliding the blade of one of the skates across his thumbnail to test its sharpness. Then he leaned over and pulled them on. He was ready for his sweater, and finally he noticed the white letter A of his new job as alternate captain had been sewed onto the red background of his sweater, near his left shoulder, above the big white N.

He looked immediately at Fat, glad for something he could kid about to take away the wounded-buck look that had come into Fat's eyes when he realized he'd started something by talking about the phone call.

"I took it up to the home economics room," Fat said.

"I'll bet you had to fight off the chicks who wanted to sew it on!" Rosy said.

"Ah!" Bill said.

"I did!"

At the back end of the dressing room, near the showers, Red Turner's hands were shoved into his jacket pockets. He listened to the by-play about Spunska's alternate-captain letter. This was some kid. If he hadn't seen it, he wouldn't have believed it himself – the driving urge that had made a hockey player out of this green kid in just one year. But the kid had been good in other sports before he took up hockey. He was that rare bird, a natural athlete with a terrific competitive spirit. He wondered, as he had often wondered before, what is it that makes us, men or boys, want so much to win a game? And he had no ready answer, buried as it was deep in the wellsprings of what makes any human being want to do something better than another. With his eyes wide open he said a little prayer asking that if these kids were to take their lumps this year, the lumps wouldn't be too big, and that in any emergencies, he, their coach, wouldn't let them down.

There was a sudden noise in the corridor, heavy thumping of skates on wood, accompanied by yells. They receded and the room was silent again. That had been Kelvin, going to the ice.

Red shoved his hat back and rubbed his hand nervously through his thinning hair. Usually he said something before a game – sometimes only a few words, sometimes some special tips about the team they were to play. He looked from one face to another, telling himself to try to say what should be said without making it corny.

"I don't have to tell you birds much," he said, walking down the room. "Just remember what you've been taught in practice. Stick to your checks. Play it as hard as you know how." He paused with one hand on the doorknob. "There's one more thing, I guess. Last year most of you were on this team when Northwest was a new school. A large part of any school is its tradition. It's just like a country. If a country's tradition is to lay down and quit everytime the going gets tough, it's not up to much. Same with a school . . ."

He paused again. A knock sounded on the door and the referee's voice called, "On the ice, you guys!"

But the coach wasn't finished. He searched in his mind for the right way to finish it. "Last year you guys didn't look as if you were up to much at the start, but you never quit – that's why you were good at the end. You, and the kids who won scholarships to the university, and the drama club, and a lot of other things at our school all helped make up what tradition Northwest now has, after only one year. You gave the school something to start on. This year I think you can do more. I think you've got a chance to give Northwest its first championship. Okay, let's go!"

They went, suddenly noisy, pounding in the corridors. Bill felt the coach's hand slap his shoulder as he passed.

And out in the corridor he was right behind when Armstrong said to Knobby Warren, "Sermons, yet!"

Bill caught the bitterness in the boy's voice. That riding of Berton's had cut deep. But why take it out this way, trying to undercut the coach? A few minutes ago Bill had been trying to protect Armstrong from further ridicule, telling Fat to shut up. But this was too much. "Lay off that stuff, Armstrong!" he said.

"Take a jump in the lake!" Armstrong retorted.

Grouchy, behind Bill, said, "What's the matter?"

But Bill wasn't going to add any more fuel than he could help, even though he was angry. "I can handle it," he said.

On the way to the ice Bill heard Grouchy's voice behind him, speaking to Pete. "I think our William is really riled."

Pete said, "First time I ever saw him mad."

In the lobby Lee Vincent and Squib Jackson finished their coffee quickly when they heard the roars from the rink that meant the first team was on the ice, and then the second. They had been chatting generally about boys who had played in this league and had gone from it to the big time. Just before they left to walk to the press box, the scout took out a notebook and jotted down names, each at the head of a blank page, Josephson and Stimers of Kelvin. Gordon, Armstrong, DeGruchy of Northwest. He hesitated at the next page, shrugged. Well, the kid was big anyway. He wrote down the name, Spunska.

CHAPTER 4 ▬

Bill hit the ice still angry at Armstrong, scarcely hearing the mixture of good-humoured boos and cheers with which the crowd greeted Northwest. Brabant was pushing the puck, black rubber with an orange core, in front of him through the Kelvin team, which was warming up. With the rest of the Northwesters, Bill followed Brabant's clumsy padded form, glancing up once to see that the bowl-like arena was nearly full, just a few seats left. Bill skated in the warm-up faster than usual, forgetting for once his self-consciousness about being a rougher skater than the others. A threat to any part of his complex hopes somehow seemed a threat to all, and Armstrong – now skating by, going the other way – was a threat. Their eyes met, exchanged glares. Bill picked up the puck and blasted a shot on goal and rounded the net hard.

Why couldn't the guy have taken it out on somebody who deserved it? One of the things all the Northwest players liked about Red Turner was that he'd never given them any hokum. What he'd said tonight was true. When Bill had started at Northwest it had had an odd aimless feeling, so new. Any talk around the halls had been about the schools the talkers had attended the year before, because there had been nothing to talk about in Northwest. And now there was – and it *was* the beginning of a tradition, and it *was* important that the beginnings of tradition should be good.

Pete skated up behind, slapped Bill's pants with the blade of his hockey stick, and said, "Cool off, there, Tiger!"

And Bill, grinning at the nickname, finally cooled off. The worst thing that could happen, he thought, would be for us to keep on arguing. He reminded himself again that Armstrong's words had been reaction to the ribbing Berton had given him. After a few games he'll be all right. I hope.

He saw Armstrong now stop at the boards and lean there, talking to his brothers, who were in a choice box seat near centre ice. Red, walking across the ice to the players' bench, spoke to him. Armstrong skated to rejoin the rest of the team.

Northwest then lined up for shots on goal, as the Kelvin team was doing at the other end of the ice. Bill's shot whacked the boards with a mighty crash. Pincher took it and scored.

Pete flicked one in. Benny Wong missed a tiny corner. . . .

There were still a few minutes to game time. The officials, dressed alike in white sweaters and dark trousers, skated the length of the ice surface, 200 feet by 85 feet, chatting, waving occasionally to someone in the crowd. The goal judges flashed tests on the red lights with which they would signal goals. The referee inspected the thick mesh draped around the metal framework of each goal, making sure there were no holes. It was all pre-game routine but it seemed to Bill to be taking an awfully long time.

Finally the referee gave a short toot on his whistle and skated to centre ice. Now things moved fast. Northwest lined up across one blueline, Kelvin across the other, all facing the flag at the end of the rink. As the lights dimmed, a mighty rustle sounded above the music as the crowd rose. The Kelvin band played "O Canada," the rest of the rink was in silence, and then the last bars of music drifted away and there was a quick released roar from the great crowd.

With a nervous turn of speed Bill skated to the bench with the other Northwest players. Red waved him back to the ice. "You and Jamieson start, kid. Keep 'em out!" Pete and Rosy and Armstrong were skating back to the ice, too, as Bill and Jamieson reached their positions on the foot-wide blueline that enclosed Northwest's defensive zone, roughly one-third of the ice surface. As he got there, Bill glanced into the stands, into the Northwest section, and saw what he was looking for – Sarah Gordon's blond hair. Her parents were on either side of her. He waved his stick. After a brief hesitation she waved in return.

"Lucky fellow," Jamieson said.

"I know it," Bill said. He had noticed her hesitation. And that it had been a very small wave. But he *was* lucky – Bill Spunska, here on the starting lineup, with this brand-new A on his sweater; his mother at the radio at home; his father, who would soon be hurrying home from night school to hear about the game. And he heard Brabant's nervous yells in the Northwest goal behind him; saw Pete and Rosy and Armstrong facing the Kelvin trio at centre ice. This year there was a new centre between Stimers and Josephson, Kelvin's two veteran wingers. Bill remembered from a write-up earlier that the centre's name was Paulson. He was about Pete's height, a little heavier, maybe. The Kelvin defence looked formidable – Mannheim and Beattie, their names were, Mannheim as big as Bill, Beattie smaller but thick in the chest.

"Hey, Gord," Bill called. "What's the Kelvin goalie's name?"

"Shewan," Jamieson said, without turning. "They say he's hot."

Shewan was slapping his pads nervously, waiting like all of them. He was tall and looked heavy in his pads as he crouched, watching centre from under the cover of his mask.

With a blast of his whistle, the referee dropped the puck between Pete and Paulson. Bill watched as Pete snared it away, passed to Armstrong on right wing. Rosy was flying for the Kelvin blueline. Armstrong flipped a long pass across and Rosy blasted a shot wildly at the Kelvin goal just as Beattie hit him with a clean, solid body check and knocked him skidding on his back into the corner.

As Kelvin's attack formed up, Bill heard Brabant in goal behind him, a never-ending nervous chant, "Come on, you guys . . . Hey Pete! Ataboy Pete, boy! Hey Rosy, go to it, Rosy. . . ."

Pete slapped the puck away from Stimers and passed again. Armstrong drove in on the Kelvin defence, head up, the puck at the end of his stick. Pete tried to slip through the defence but was blocked, and Armstrong fired a shot at the Kelvin goal. Shewan kicked it away. Paulson scooted behind his goal to pick up the puck.

Pete was still in behind the Kelvin blueline. As Paulson made his break to get out, Pete slapped the puck back into the corner and dashed in after it. But Mannheim got there first and flipped a pass out to the blueline. Then Kelvin's hottest line was pounding in on the Northwest defence. Just like in the dream, Bill thought. Now! Paulson flew in from nowhere and yelled, cutting in to centre, and took a pass. Bill threw a body check and hit him hard, but Stimers rushed in and got the puck and when Bill turned to get back into the play, Stimers was working his way in on goal. Pete hooked it loose and tried to get out but Paulson, with a sweeping check, got it back, and then Jamieson hit him.

Jamieson, a thin fair boy, tall but not heavy, wasn't a noted body checker. But this time Paulson seemed off balance just for an instant after getting the puck back from Pete. Bill saw Gord's shoulders and chest thrust forward as he hit Paulson squarely and the puck bounced free, to Bill.

With a yell he turned and dashed down the ice. First game, first chance, show 'em! He charged toward the Kelvin blueline, seeing big Mannheim waiting for him, hearing yells from each side of him, one from Armstrong and one from Pete, placing themselves for his pass as Rosy stayed back to cover for Bill. At the last instant Bill glanced to the left to make sure it was Pete who had yelled and not some Kelvin player trying to draw a blind pass. It was Pete, all right, flying, and Bill tapped the puck over to that wing, aiming it ten feet ahead of Pete, and he made this pass just as he got within reach of Mannheim. He tried to avoid the crashing check, tried a shift, but he kept himself tense, too, and the crash as the two hit was like an explosion in his ears as they both went down. But as he hit the ice he could see Pete cutting in on goal from left wing, the other defenceman trying to outwait him, the goalie crouched to cover that side. Then, scrambling to his feet again to get back to his position, Bill saw Pete's cool pass across to Armstrong and the blazing quick shot. Shewan sprang full length, mitted hand outstretched, and knocked it into the corner. Whatever was the matter with Armstrong, it disappeared when the whistle went. He was good.

Bill dug in and got back to his own blueline, happy that the rush had been a good one, turning on the heat. But Kelvin was coming back again.

"Watch the pass!" Bill yelled and moved toward the wing to get Josephson. The Kelvin winger passed back to Paulson. He dropped his shoulder for a shot, using the onrushing Jamieson as a screen, and let go. Brabant kicked it out. Bill had dashed back to the front of the net, was there for the rebound, passed out to

Pete, and the play spun down into the Kelvin end again.

But this time Rosy got across Kelvin's blueline ahead of the puck, offside. The referee blew his whistle to stop play. Over the boards from the Northwest bench jumped Hurry Berton, stocky centre for Northwest's second line. With him were the Chief and chunky little Alec Mitchell. Then came the new defence, Warren and DeGruchy. Complete change. Bill and Jamieson followed Pete's line to the bench.

"These guys are good," Pete said, beside Bill, as Fat threw towels around their necks against the perspiration that was running from their faces and scalps after that first burst of action.

"Nice going, gents," Red called from behind them, along the bench.

"Armstrong," Rosy said, "that was a ferocious shot of yours. That Shewan was good to stop it."

"Just lucky," Armstrong said.

Then there was something to watch on the ice.

"Hey, look at that little guy go!" Pete said.

They looked. There was no need for further identification. The right winger on Kelvin's second line, a new boy to the league, was moving away from Mitchell, his check, as if Mitchell were standing still. The Kelvin wing was the smallest man on the ice, short, light, and with a stiff-legged skating style, short strides, immense speed.

Red yelled along the bench. "Hey, Fat! Who's that?"

"Lorne Zubek," Fat called. "They call him Zingo."

"They should!" Pete said.

It was almost funny to see the contortions Mitch was going through now to keep up to the little guy, now that he'd shown that one burst of speed. But Mitchell managed to stick with him, or close to him, and keep him away from the Northwest net. He came off mopping his brow, looking shaken.

Then Bill and Jamieson went back on, with Pincher Martin's line. And Pincher took over. Always a great opportunist, he caught the Kelvin third-string centre loafing behind Kelvin's blueline, snared the puck away from him, blasted a quick shot on goal. Shewan dove to bat it out. Benny Wong got the rebound. Shewan did the splits to make the save, kicked it into the corner. Scotty McIntosh was in fast, outfought his check and a defenceman, got a pass out front to Pincher.

Pincher back-handed a fast one. Shewan stopped it with his stick. But Pincher was there for his own rebound. With the Kelvin centre checking him from one side and the Kelvin defenceman from the other, he managed to get another fast shot away. And this time Shewan got only a piece of it. Couldn't block it . . . and it was in!

Bill, at the Kelvin blueline, jumped in the air as the red light signalled the goal. Then he dashed in and slammed Pincher on the back.

"Nice going, Pincher!" he yelled. "Nice going, boy!

"Hit me like that again and I'll probably never get another one," said Pincher, when he got his wind back.

When the teams left the ice for the first ten-minute rest the score hadn't changed from that 1-0 for Northwest.

On the ice, off the ice, checking, rushing, passing, the rhythm of the game catching him up, Bill scarcely noticed the passing of time through the second period. Northwest had about three-quarters of the play but couldn't get it past the acrobatic Shewan again.

Then in the third period Kelvin clicked.

Bill was on the bench when it started. Mannheim, deep in the Kelvin zone, got the puck. Zubek was wheeling near the blueline. He was away like a flash, Mitch caught two steps behind him. Mannheim's long pass hit Zubek at centre. Then they really saw some speed. Zubek went around Warren almost before Knobby could move, leaped in the air to avoid

Grouchy's smashing check an instant later, and was in all alone, stick dancing, hips swinging. It was too much for Brabant. He stared as if spellbound for a second, then made his move. Too soon. As the rest of the Northwests got back, Zubek hit the top of the net with a perfect flick shot, and skated back down the ice with the crowd on its feet cheering for a great scoring effort.

Kelvin 1, Northwest 1.

Mitchell banged his stick on the ice in disgust on the way to the bench. Bill, coming to the ice, wanted to say something to cheer him up, but couldn't. They'd outplayed Kelvin for nearly the whole game and now had lost their lead. His emotion surprised him. It seemed something entirely outside of him. "Let's get it back!" he yelled to Gord, to Pete, to Rosy, even to Armstrong. But the Kelvin team, fired by this goal, stormed all around Brabant. Bill held his teeth together so tight that they hurt as the Kelvins charged in on him again and again. He glanced at the clock in one lull. Six minutes to play. The team that got a goal now would have an overwhelming advantage, a goal up and only a few minutes to play. He knocked Paulson down. Then Mannheim. Then Beattie. Then Stimers. He even managed once to check Zubek. In the press box Squib Jackson gave Lee Vincent a stiff body check simultaneously with Bill's last one.

The roar of the crowd was constant now and Bill's breath was coming hard and he was checking, checking, determined that whoever got the goal that would break the tie wouldn't do it through him.

Paulson was coming in again. Bill set himself for a body check, saw the puck get away from Paulson, poked at it suddenly, sent it free into the centre zone, raced after it.

The Kelvin forward line had been caught out of position, going the other way. So had the Northwest line, skating stride for stride with them. Bill was alone, getting up speed with that quick, rough, powerful stride that always brought the crowd to its feet. He saw the defence spread a little to be ready if he tried to go around them, and made his decision. He went at the hole between them. They came together. He felt their sticks. He bounced off Mannheim into Beattie and then was through, the puck before him, half off balance, the screaming uproar of the crowd in his ears; and he hauled back and blasted a shot at an open corner. Shewan stabbed at it, touched it, couldn't hold it, and as Beattie came back and crashed him to the ice Bill saw the goal judge's red light flash on.

Then Pete was on him, grabbing him around the shoulders, hugging him. "That's your first one, boy! The first of hundreds!" The Berton line was coming to the ice and the Chief patted Bill hard on the behind as he went by. On the bench everybody was yelling back and forth about Bill's first goal and Bill sat there grinning around knowing that he never had felt better in his life.

And that goal turned the tide. It lifted the Northwest team. They stormed all around the Kelvin goal. They couldn't beat Shewan again. He was magnificent. But Brabant was magnificent, too. The few times Kelvin got through on him from then on, he saved coolly.

The Northwest fans almost blasted the roof off as the final buzzer sounded and the Northwest team skated from the rink. Fat jauntily carried the sticks across the ice and followed the others to the dressing room. Red came last, knowing that this year he had another hockey team.

Up in the lobby with Pete a little later, Bill looked for Sarah. Last year when Northwest played the early game she'd usually come to the lobby after, to join Pete and Bill, then together they would find seats for the second game. But they couldn't see her.

"Come on," Pete said. "Let's go and see. Maybe she's holding seats for us. Big crowd tonight."

They walked along the corridor under the

seats and came up through a passageway to where they could see the ice, just as St. John's and Daniel Mac started their game. But when they looked up to where the Gordons and Sarah were sitting there was only one extra seat.

"You take it, Pete," Bill said, "I see a seat up higher."

Pete started to protest, but Bill already was on his way. And in the middle of the next game, with St. John's ahead 3-0, he started thinking that he'd have to set the alarm for seven in the morning, so he could be in to work at eight. He left quietly and walked through the empty lobby to catch a bus alone.

CHAPTER 5 ■

Bill arrived at Desmond's the next morning at quarter to eight and found the door locked and no one else there. He stepped into the doorway out of the north wind, which was blowing icy particles in swirls and eddies on the frozen street. First day at work. It was a funny feeling. He couldn't help thinking that if he didn't have this job he'd still be in a warm bed, maybe waking about now, thinking about what good things could be done with this day. He wished now, though, that he'd told Pete last night about this job. Waiting for Sarah had been a mistake.

A man swung down the street from the bus stop. He was erect, slim, middle-aged, with a big mustache, and he marched as if carrying a rifle past a covey of generals. He stopped at the door, fishing for a key.

"You're the new kid," this man said.

"Yes, sir."

"I'm Albert Fowler, the shipper. Call me Albert. What's your name?"

"Bill Spunska, sir."

Albert chuckled and said, "Lay off that 'sir' stuff. Call me Albert, I said." He opened the door. "Come on, I'll show you around."

Albert led the way back through the empty office, opened a door in a wall-to-wall glass partition, and then they were in a long room crowded with shelves piled high with every kind of cigarettes and tobacco Bill ever had heard of, and dozens more. Some of the shelves were against the wall, ceiling high. Others holding other goods ran lengthwise down the warehouse. Albert's brisk manner made Bill lose some of his shyness as he was led up and down the aisles, Albert talking a mile a minute.

By the time they got back to the front office it suddenly had come alive. Albert introduced him around and Bill felt the appraisal in the eyes of the four salesmen, two phone girls, and credit manager. The bookkeeper Bill had seen at the computer when he came in yesterday said a friendly "Hello." When they got back to the warehouse there was a pounding on the back door and Albert admitted a boy a little older than Bill, dark and small and quick. He was Herbie Hughes, the assistant shipper. In another minute, two big breezy young men came in at the back, shouting hellos. They were Don and Gerry Fitzpatrick, brothers, and they drove the trucks.

them together, and pushed his fur hat back on his head. "Well, look sharp there, boy," he said, "I'm a customer."

Albert came from the front of the warehouse, banging his feet down in that military way. "Hi there, kid," he called to Grouchy. "Guess you know this guy, eh?"

"Sure do," Grouchy said. "Hey, Albert, you got some of that big slab chocolate with the peanuts in it? We need a case. I was going by so I thought I'd drop in and save your trucks a trip."

"Sure thing, kid," Albert said, marching off to his desk. "I'll write out an order."

Bill considered asking Grouchy not to say anything about this. He reconsidered immediately. That would be silly. He didn't like senseless secrets, and that's what this would be. Grouchy wouldn't rush right out and phone Pete and Sarah anyway. He found the pipe cleaners, finishing that order, and came back to the door again to say "So long" to Grouchy. Grouchy jerked his head at Bill, beckoning him aside.

"You keeping this quiet or something?" Grouchy asked.

Bill shook his head. "Just got the job yesterday," he said. "Didn't have time to tell anybody, yet."

"I wondered where you were last night after

the second game," Grouchy said. "Saw Pete and Sarah having hot chocolate with guess who!"

"Who?"

"Armstrong!"

Bill must have looked very startled, because Grouchy laughed. "Better not relax, boy," he said. "He was doing all right, looked like to me!"

Then, on his way out, something seemed to occur to Grouchy. He dropped his light manner, abruptly, as he turned. "Something I meant to say," he said. "For the good of the team, we've gotta get along with that guy." He was talking as Northwest's captain now and Bill knew it.

"I know," Bill said.

"See you Monday," Grouchy said.

As Grouchy walked up the ramp and out the back door, Bill kept on going, forgetting for an instant the kind of canned goods he was looking for and catching himself not thinking of work at all. Armstrong! He read the invoice again, found the cases, walked back to the big tables where orders were packed, then picked up another order to fill.

At twelve o'clock there was a lull. The tables were loaded with orders ready to be carried to the delivery trucks. The Fitzpatricks, knocking snow from their feet, stamped in through the back door a few minutes apart. Both headed downstairs to the coffee room to eat. Herbie followed them. Albert was eating his lunch at his desk. At his elbow were two phones. Bill didn't relish talking with Albert sitting right there, but now that Grouchy knew, he felt it had to be done. It was Pete as well as Sarah, he insisted to himself. But neither of them should hear about this from someone else.

"Could I use one of the phones?" he asked.

"Sure thing, kid." Albert shoved one over and picked up his lunch. "I'll go down for some coffee. If the other phone rings, stop talking to your girl and answer it. Check?"

Bill had to grin. "Right," he said.

He was grateful to Albert for leaving. It was odd, the way he felt. What if Sarah answered? Would he ask for Pete? He hadn't even got this sorted out in his mind when the phone was ringing at the other end. And Sarah answered.

"It's Bill," he said.

"Oh." Her voice was cool.

He didn't plan the words. They just came. When he phoned, he hadn't even been thinking of that argument with Sarah yesterday. But between the time she said "Hello" and ten seconds later it all came in a rush. "I wanted to apologize for being short with you yesterday," he said. "I didn't mean to. But there was something I couldn't tell you then. I was going out to look for a job and I knew that if I got it I wouldn't have time to be of much use to the dramatic society. But I didn't mean to be rude."

"You should have told me!"

"I hadn't even told my parents, then," Bill said, and as he explained it all now the strain gradually went, the old easiness coming back, and he was glad.

Sarah said, "That was a neat goal you got last night. I just about died, I yelled so hard."

"I thought maybe you'd be too mad at me to yell."

"Don't be silly. I couldn't get that mad."

Bill felt as if he'd been carrying a load of stone on his shoulders all morning and it suddenly had been removed. They were talking at a great rate, all tension gone, when he heard chairs scrape back downstairs and it suddenly occurred to him that tonight he'd be paid, and since Dad refused to take all of it, he'd have some for himself. He never had asked Sarah even to a movie in the year they'd known one another. He'd never felt he had the money. Buses and lunchtime milk took most of what he could make shovelling snow and doing other odd jobs.

"Sarah," he said, "I've just got a minute now,

but I'll be finished at six, and I wondered . . . Would you go to a movie with me, or skating, or something, tonight?"

He'd never really thought of them as steadies, because they weren't. Sometimes if Pete and Bill and some others played bridge on a Saturday night Sarah went skating or to a movie with other friends, male or female. . . . Still Bill had a sinking feeling when Sarah paused just a second or two, then said, "I'm awfully sorry, Bill, but I told Cliff Armstrong I'd go out with him tonight. I just didn't know . . ."

Albert and Herbie and the Fitzpatricks were upstairs now, coming closer, all looking at Bill on the phone. Albert banged his hands together and said, "Let's get this load out!"

"Maybe another time," Sarah said.

"I've got to go now," Bill said unhappily.

"I'll tell Pete about your job," she said brightly, but now the brightness didn't seem as warm to Bill.

"Good-bye, then," Bill said, and she said good-bye. He hung up and got up from the desk.

Albert, close to him, chuckled. "Don't take it so hard, boy!" he said. "She'll go out with you next time, maybe. . . . Now you go and eat." He grabbed a pushcart, loaded it with parcels and pushed it up the ramp to the loading entrance, singing, soulfully, "All alo-o-o-one, by the telepho-o-o-one . . ."

Bill went down the rough wooden staircase to the basement. It was dark but he walked toward a light at the front end and made it without tripping on the big mounds of cases stacked on the floor. The lunchroom was simply a long clean table and a two-burner plate for coffee.

He was almost always hungry. Now his sandwiches tasted like damp cardboard. He drank milk he'd bought earlier when a milkman called at the back door of the warehouse. It didn't taste right, either. After a few minutes he went back upstairs and grabbed a pushcart, too. He worked hard at loading the trucks and then at filling more orders, and eventually the press of steady slugging work for the rest of the day pushed everything else to the back of his mind.

CHAPTER 6 ▬

It was amazing how quickly the word got around the school that before the Kelvin game there had been words between Berton and Armstrong, then between Spunska and Armstrong. And before the gossip had a chance to slow down it got another good prod, in public.

Anything that was said at the hockey team's table could be heard at other tables nearby, and Monday noon when they were all about half through eating lunch Rosy looked around and said, "Hey, where's Armstrong?"

Pete said, "My sister conned him into joining the dramatic society. Seems they need a guy for the lead in the play they're going to put on. They're meeting right now in the auditorium and eating their lunches in there."

Bill dropped his sandwich and picked it up in confusion.

Brabant called down from the end of the table, "What play are they doing?"

"*Life with Father,*" Pete said.

Rosy chuckled. "I saw that. Aha! Good

casting! This father, he is a man always arguing. Pigheaded. For Armstrong, it will not be
like acting at all. . . ."

Alec Mitchell put down his milk and his normally mild face got red. "Shouldn't talk about a
guy when he isn't here," he said.

"I would say the same if he was here," Rosy
said.

Mitch sputtered a little. "All right, you guys
don't like him! The whole darn bunch of you
are nuts! He can't help what his brothers do.
Berton, you should realize that. You've got
your knife into him, Spunska's got his knife into
him. . . ."

Grouchy said, "Shut up, Mitch! You know we
just keep Rosy around for the laughs. If he'd
said that about someone else nobody would
have cared."

"But it wasn't about someone else," Mitch
said.

Stretch got into it. "If he can't take some kidding, to his face or behind his back, he won't
last long on any team."

Bill said abruptly, "And I haven't got my
knife into him, Mitch."

"How about the other night before the
game?"

"That's over," Bill said. "He had no right to
say what he said."

"I don't know what he said, but maybe he was

just joking, too, like Rosy," Mitch said a little sarcastically.

"Ask him what he said," Bill said.

"Break it up!" Grouchy ordered. "Cut it out."

They finished lunch in silence, and as he was eating Bill forgot about what had been said later and thought about what had started it all – that Armstrong was in the dramatic society. He'd worked fast. Of course, the chance was tailor-made. And probably Sarah was the feminine lead.

Bill had a mental picture of Sarah and Armstrong saying lines to one another in the school auditorium late each afternoon while he hunted for pipe cleaners and chocolate bars down at Desmond's. It was an unpleasant comparison.

Probably Mitch reported that lunchtime conversation to Armstrong, because antagonism that previously had been felt rather than seen now came out in the open. Armstrong tried a few verbal jabs with Rosy but Rosy refused to take him seriously, replying, "Yes, Father," and "No, Father," and "You know best, Father," to everything he said. Berton's acid tongue was an uncomfortable adversary, too. At least, that's how it seemed to Bill – that Armstrong now was concentrating all his needling on him. They were about the same size, same weight, and they were both tough hockey players. The team began to watch the feud grow. In workouts they body-checked each other, played it hard, and Armstrong always put on his best shift coming in on Bill and sometimes made him look bad. Then he'd rib Bill's rough skating by calling him Ice Follies. One time after Bill had made a particularly fine rush in a workout Rosy had told him he looked just like Bobby Orr. Bill didn't even know who Bobby Orr was. Rosy, as shocked as if Bill had confessed that he didn't know the world was round, explained that Bobby Orr had been the greatest defenceman of them all. "I saw him once when I was a little kid, down East," Rosy said. "Honest, that time you looked just like him!" Armstrong, listening, said, "Yeah, if Orr wore snowshoes instead of skates."

The tension grew in small ways as well as large. Bill dropped into the auditorium one snowy noon to watch rehearsals of the play. He didn't enjoy it. Armstrong, in the fat role of Father, and Sarah, as the somewhat scatter-brained, devious mother, looked to be having too much fun. From the dark at the back of the auditorium he saw something else, too, which he had half suspected. Armstrong was acting two parts. One was the formal one of Father. The other was a part, too – a polite, obliging young man whenever Sarah was around. Pete had told Bill that Sarah couldn't understand at all why the team didn't get along with Armstrong. No wonder.

Bill wasn't sure just when people outside of the school began to hear about it. But it wasn't more than a week later. Friday night Northwest swamped St. John's Tech 7-1. The following noon Bill was eating lunch downstairs at Desmond's, thinking that tonight he and Dad would sit down together again and knock more off that debt arrears total, when Albert marched along the basement toward him, carrying his lunch. "Finished, kid?"

"Just going up," Bill said.

"Don't hurry. Herbie's up there. Say, what's this I hear about trouble on your team?"

Bill stared at him. "Why? What do you hear?"

"There's a sergeant in our outfit in the reserve army has a kid on your team. Jack Mitchell, the guy's name is."

"Sure," Bill said. "Alec Mitchell is his son, I guess."

"Jack says his kid tells him that there's some trouble between one of the new kids on the team and some guys who were on it last year."

Bill's first impulse was to tell Albert that no such trouble existed. But that was just wishful thinking. It did exist. He shrugged. "There is a little trouble, I guess. But it hasn't hurt the team, yet."

He went back upstairs. It hasn't hurt the team, *yet*. But as he picked up an order and started touring the shelves to fill it, he had to grin when he thought of what would have happened to Armstrong if he'd been with the team last year, Grouchy's first as captain. Last year Grouchy had been the kind of a captain who told people off very quickly if they didn't act the way he thought they should. This year was different. He was handling Armstrong with kid gloves. Maybe that was the only way. He knew Grouchy didn't like Armstrong's attitude any more than anyone else did. Last year he would have shown it. This year he did his best to hide it. Bill wondered if one of the secrets of leadership was to be able to get along at least outwardly with people like Armstrong.

Then it got into the paper, because the crowd booed Northwest the night they beat Daniel McIntyre 5-1 for their third straight win.

The Sunday morning two days after that game Bill woke with a start. His father was standing in the doorway of his bedroom, and in the soft grey light of the winter morning Bill sat up quickly, rubbing his eyes, and then was half out of bed before he remembered. He sank back on the pillow.

"Sunday . . ." he said. "Wonderful day."

His father came into the room, glanced around, and settled on the edge of the bed to thumb a new book Bill had got from the school library. Their relationship was a good one. After years apart there had been a kind of constraint between them. They just didn't know one another well enough to assume a father-son relationship immediately and without strain. For a year they had been feeling more and more at ease, but Bill's job had made the final difference. Now that both of them were working extra hours to get the family on its feet they had a shared purpose which never had been so well defined as it was now.

"What time is it?" Bill asked.

"About nine-thirty."

"Boy, that was a good sleep!" Bill stretched out luxuriously, pushing his feet up against the end of the bed. "Mother still asleep?"

"Just went down."

Sunday was the one day in the week when no one dressed for breakfast. Later they probably would go to church together, but even that wasn't a rule. Last week they had all slept so long that they hadn't got to church at all. There were no rules for Sundays.

"Did you get a chance to read the paper when you came in last night?" Bill's father asked.

Bill hadn't been home for dinner. Last night

80

he and Pete and Win Kryschuk, a player from last year's team, now in pre-med at the university, had played bridge at Pincher Martin's place. They played intent bridge, not much talking, but when they were having Cokes later they'd talked some about a story in Lee Vincent's column. "I read it yesterday at work. You meant the stuff about them booing us?"

Dad nodded. "An odd way for people to react."

Bill didn't answer. It was queer that Northwest, the crowd's favourite last year when they were underdogs, had been booed at times in their last two games. There hadn't been any in the Kelvin game. But that had been close. The next two games had been different. Northwest had piled up a 7–0 lead before St. John's even got into the scoring at all. Then they'd run wild again, against Daniel Mac.

The paper was beside the bed. Bill reached down and felt for it. It was folded to Lee's column, which, under his picture, was headed "Lee Vincent Says" . . .

I don't remember a time in hockey when a crowd has switched so rapidly from liking a team to disliking it as has been the case with Northwest's entry in the Inter-High hockey league. Part of it, of course, is the crowd's constant desire to see a favourite beaten. But it isn't all that, in this case.

Last year the crowd liked Northwest because

apart from one player – Pete Gordon – nobody had ever heard of the boys who became Northwest stars. Another appealing thing about the team was that none of these boys who were stars by the end of the season seemed to realize that they *had* become stars. They just got out there and dug in and never quit. Early in the season they were constantly out-played, and yet they were never easy to beat. When they got clicking later they had to win four straight to complete the sensational rise from last place into the playoffs. But they did it. This year they already seem to be shoo-ins for the playoffs and yet oddly enough there doesn't seem to be, about the team, the same feeling of everybody giving everything which was the main strength of last year's team.

There have been some rumours as to why this is so. One rumour is that the new boys on the team, particularly Cliff Armstrong, feel that the veterans of last year have things too much their own way in running the team. For instance, Armstrong believes he's a better centre than a winger. He was a centre last year at Brandon. But my recollection of that team is that it wasn't particularly Armstrong at centre that made it strong, but that the team was in good harmony, Armstrong part of it. Anyway, he's leading the league in goals with five in three games so he can't be too badly misplaced.

His presence on that line is even more important than the goals he scores, too. He's taken the heat off Pete Gordon. Last year Gordon was that line's main scoring threat and the opposition concentrated on stopping him. This year if they stop Gordon, Armstrong scores; if they stop Armstrong, Gordon scores. If they stop them both, Buchanan scores. And nobody, so far, has been able to stop them both at the same time. That scoring punch, combined with a fine defence, has put Northwest where it is today – three games, three victories, with fourteen goals against the opposition's measly three. But I wonder, do all those goals, and all those wins, make up for the loss of last year's cheers? And I wonder if those Northwesters know that it is possible to win and be popular too.

Bill dropped the paper on the floor again. "The trouble is, he's right."

"Right about what?" Dad asked, picking up the paper himself and glancing at Lee's column again.

"*I* don't even like the way the team acts sometimes," Bill said. "Wrangling half the time."

"Have you any theories as to what makes Armstrong act this way?"

Bill hoisted himself up on one elbow. He had theories. He'd been thinking about this affair a lot. "I think it's his brothers," he said. "As far as anybody knows, he didn't act this way last year when he was living at home in Brandon, away from these brothers. But they've got quite a bit of money – a wholesale clothing business – and I guess they just dote on Cliff. One of them told our coach that the reason they'd had Cliff come here was they didn't figure his coach at Brandon last year was good enough!" Bill had heard that from Fat. Sarah had verified it. She knew Armstrong better than any of them. It gave Bill a pang to think of that, but she'd told Pete that Armstrong had said once, half jokingly, but not all, that if he didn't make it as a professional star, his brothers would never forgive him. Bill told Dad that now.

Dad looked serious. "That's a lot of pressure for a boy to carry."

As Bill went to the bathroom he could smell the good smells of the big Sunday breakfast coming up from the kitchen. He sloshed water on his face and couldn't put away the sort of sad feeling that he got every time he thought of some aspects of this year's team. Sure, it was good to win three in a row. If they could win them all, then the playoffs, then the provincial final with Brandon or Portage la Prairie or whoever won out there, that would be wonderful. . . . But would it? No matter what it was that made Armstrong act the way he did, the fact was that he did act that way, and it spoiled a lot of things. He pulled on his dressing gown and some thick socks and headed down the stairs.

He liked the look of his mother in the morning better than other times of the day, pale without make-up, but cheerful and smiling and somehow comfortable. It was family custom to eat a big breakfast. Especially on Sunday. On the ancient electric stove one frying pan was full of bacon. Another was ready for the eggs. A pot of coffee percolated on a back burner. His mother, in a warm red dressing gown, smiled as Bill hugged her shoulders. Then she ground pepper into the scrambled eggs, added chopped onions and said, "You two sit down."

Mr. Spunska went to the sink to rinse off his hands and Bill sat down on one of the painted wooden chairs. This one's legs were braced with wire. The oilcloth on the table was scrubbed clean. The cupboards against the inside wall were painted to match the chairs. It was amazing what paint and oilcloth had done for the dirty old pile of kitchen furniture Bill and his father had carted in here not much more than a year ago now from a truck sent around from the secondhand store.

Dad sat down, poured himself a cup of coffee, and began to sip it. He liked it steaming hot. "How's the work now?" he asked.

"Fine," Bill said. He told them about work for a while. They spent nearly the next hour over breakfast. Then, full to the brim, Bill got up and stretched. Through the window he could see scattered small flakes of snow falling. And it looked cold.

He decided not to get dressed just yet. Might spend the whole day mostly on his back. To heck with what people said, and what the paper said, and to heck with Armstrong. He'd be all right. Everything would be all right.

CHAPTER 7

When Bill got to the rink for hockey practice three days later, he felt like one of the Eskimo hunters in a book he'd been reading. He was sure the Barren Lands couldn't be colder than this. The thermometer at the school said the temperature was minus thirty. That wasn't the coldest it would get that winter by a long shot, but a wind was howling out of the north and in the seven-block walk through the frozen streets he'd had his collar up to protect his cheeks and the fur flaps on his hat down over his ears. The rink seemed as cold as the outside. But the dressing room was warm enough. About half the team was there. Bill tucked his mitts under his arm and held his hands over the hot-air register, looking around.

"What's the matter, boy?" Fat asked. "Doesn't it get cold in Poland?"

"Not this cold, I hope," Bill said. "Or if it does I'm glad we don't live there any more."

"This isn't cold," Fat said. "Practically Indian summer."

Rosy came in and heard the last of that. "In that case," he said, taking up a position beside Bill at the stove, "we should have from our only Indian a comment. Hey, Chief?"

"Ugh," commented the Chief.

They began to change for the workout, gossiping a little about the games last night, Tuesday, when a double-header had been played so the league's first-half games could be finished before the Christmas holidays. Gordon Bell had scraped through with a 4–3 win over Daniel Mac, but St. John's had shown surprising strength to hold Kelvin to a 2–2 tie. Kelvin's only loss in three games now had been to Northwest, and by that narrow one-goal margin. Gordon Bell's only loss in three starts had been to Kelvin, another 2–1 affair, and this Friday Northwest would face Gordon Bell. Lots of gab material for the team's talkers in all that, since if Gordon Bell won, they'd tie Northwest for first place.

Every time the door opened and closed the draft from the corridor swept through the room. Soon every time some one came in the others chorused, "Close the door!" And eventually they did it to Armstrong. Since being named by Lee Vincent as the main disturbing influence on the team, Armstrong hadn't eaten with the others at school. Rosy, who was in the same room as Armstrong, along with Mitchell and Berton, said he'd been going home for lunch on the days when there were no noon rehearsals. Now Armstrong closed the door with a bang that made Red Turner look up quickly from his seat on the equipment trunk at the end of the room. And Red also noticed that Armstrong had been almost the last man to arrive. Only one missing now was the spare goalie, Rod McElroy. In fifteen minutes the team was due on the ice. Red wondered what had happened to McElroy.

Most of the team took Armstrong's door slam in silence, but not Rosy.

"Watch out there, Armstrong," he said. "You want to make the rink fall down?"

"You told me to close the door," Armstrong said.

"All right! All right!" Fat said, to stop the bickering. Fat was given to being slightly bossy. Most of the team didn't mind. Fat had a lot to do, in his job as equipment manager, and usually he got the tolerance from the rest of the team that athletes usually give to a boy who would like to be an athlete but who, through size or some other factor, can't quite make it.

"What's that mean?" Armstrong said. He still had the chip on his shoulder.

Bill stifled a tart reply.

"It just means all right, all right," Pincher said, from the corner near the showers. "Let it go at that."

There was a knock at the door, and one of the rink rats opened it, a swarthy youngster who helped with the ice-cleaning. "You're wanted on the phone, Mr. Turner," he said.

Red raised his eyebrows and followed the rink rat out.

Then Jamieson produced a minor sensation. Solemnly, he took from his pocket a pair of horn-rimmed spectacles, put them on, and taped them to his temples.

As boy after boy noticed what he was doing, gradually the noise in the dressing room rose to a crescendo of questions. And Jamieson explained that he'd been having headaches at shows. His mother has sent him to the doctor, who sent him to an eye specialist.

"Hence the cheaters!" Pincher said.

"Hence, indeed," Jamieson agreed.

"But won't it be dangerous, wearing them on the ice?"

"I don't think so. . . . The doc said it might even make me play better. Now that I can see people I'll be able to hit 'em better."

"So you guys look out for your jobs," Grouchy said to Spunska, Warren and Rosy.

Red apparently had known about the spectacles. When he returned he paid no attention to them. He looked unhappy.

"That was McElroy," he said. "He's been trying to get me. I've been out of the office all day. His father has been transferred to Newfoundland. They're leaving right away. Got a chance to go in an air force plane."

"No spare goalie," Grouchy said thoughtfully, looking around the room.

"Bad break," Red said. "I was figuring the best way to get back in shape after that layoff was to spend the whole hour scrimmaging." He looked at Ward, Somerset and Michaluk, who had been working out with the team all season but hadn't yet made it in a game. "Any of you boys ever play goal?"

They all shook their heads.

Red looked around the room. Suddenly he grinned. "Fat," he said, "Here's your big chance."

The ludicrous look on Fat's face made everybody laugh. He stood there in the corner, his mouth half open, one finger pointing to his chest, gulping. "Me?" he said finally.

"We will hire a rink rat to help you lift your leg each time you're to make a save, Fat!" said Rosy.

Fat recovered. "I'll lift 'em, all right!" He whipped out of his clothes. Bill, watching him, thought it was sort of sad, in a way, that a boy who obviously wanted so much to be a player got his chance only when there was no one else to turn to.

"Don't take it too seriously, there, boy," Red said, maybe noticing what Bill had seen.

Rosy said, "Nobody is allowed to score more than ten goals on Fat."

"I know one guy who won't get a goal on me," Fat said, "and that's you, rubber stick."

Red, listening to the kidding, thought maybe this was a good thing. The dressing room had been uncomfortable, before. Bill and Pete helped Fat on with his pads, tightening straps until Fat yelped, yanking the belly pad and sweater over his head as if they were dressing a doll. And each time Fat came up for air he had this happy look on his face. "Good thing you guys have got me," he said, two or three times. "Utility man."

Rosy said, "You will serve us the same purpose as the dummy serves for soldiers who have bayonet practice."

"I'm warning you, Rosy," Fat said, "I'm going to shut you out." He was enjoying the banter. As equipment manager, he was almost as much a member of the team as anyone, but he loved this break in the routine of counting sweaters and issuing laces and tape.

Red picked up the white slipovers that would

identify one of the pickup teams in the scrimmage. He tossed one to Fat, others to Rosy, Bill, the Berton line, and the Martin line. Rosy groaned that now he wouldn't get a chance to score ten on Fat. Bill could see the logic in it. Fat would get a good defence and two regular lines. Brabant would get the other defence and the first line, but also the three untried kids, Ward, Somerset and Michaluk. Then the Northwest players swarmed out of the dressing room and over the boards to the fresh ice, unmarked because it hadn't been used since its flooding earlier in the day.

Bill and Rosy skated back with Fat to the goal and got him turned around facing the right way. Fat had a grin on his face that wouldn't come off. "What I want is a shutout," he said, as he pulled on his goal mask. "I don't want any defencemen backing in too close, or any of that kind of stuff, either."

"Yes, sir," Bill said.

Red was tooting his whistle at centre ice. Pete was there, with Buchanan and Armstrong on his wings; Grouchy and Warren behind them; Brabant in goal. The Berton line was starting in front of Bill and Rosy for the Whites.

"Let's just see how long we can keep those guys from getting a shot on goal," Rosy said. Bill grinned. Rosy, for all his kidding, had felt the undertone of serious hope in Fat and wanted to help him make some kind of a creditable showing.

"He's a darn good sport to go in there, that Fat, that's all," Rosy said, defending his sentiment.

The workout started out calmly enough, all business. Red skated up and down with the play, yelling to correct mistakes, sometimes stopping play to talk for a minute to a player. Then it began to warm up and Red made fewer and fewer interruptions as the first half hour went by. The lines were changing fairly frequently, the defence getting only the rest given them by Jamieson's spelling off each one in turn, on both sides. Bill was breathing hard, but it was a good exertion, made him feel good because he'd played it hard and he was still fairly fresh. The Three Ghosts were having the times of their lives. So was Fat. He fanned on one long shot, but Rosy and Bill had kept most attackers away. Pincher Martin had scored one on Brabant, too. The score was 1-1 when Red stopped play momentarily to demonstrate to Bill and Rosy how to come out on the blueline, fairly close together, to meet a three-man rush.

"Close up the centre," he said, "make the guy pass. . . . Be ready to get back as soon as the pass is made, but if you can make him pass to the wings maybe it'll be a bad pass, maybe our back checkers will get it, maybe it'll put somebody offside – and even if none of those happens, it's better to have a winger with the puck, coming in from a bad angle, than having a guy coming right down centre." He was finished, and Bill was tucking that one away to work on, when he saw Armstrong's brothers come into the rink and sit beside the players' bench. Armstrong went over to speak to them. They had another couple of men with them. Berton had taken that interval to duck off the ice for a minute. He came back over the boards just then, and said to Bill as he went by, "Guess what? The men behind the throne have brought friends to see what a hot-shot Cliffy is. . . . And him with only Fat to beat! He'll be a ruddy hero!"

Before, Armstrong had seemed content to go along with Red's suggestion that everybody go easy on Fat. Bill wondered how he'd react now. He was always harder to handle with his brothers around. And now, with someone his brothers wanted to impress watching too, what would he do?

The answer came fast. Pete got the face-off and passed to Armstrong, speeding up the wing. Armstrong skated straight at Spunska, executed a fast double shift that left Spunska at the blueline untangling his legs, and went in to beat Fat with a rising shot to a top corner – exactly the same kind of a shot he would have tried on an experienced goaler, without regard for the fact that if such a shot was off line, or too high, and went for Fat's face, Fat's reflexes weren't good enough to be sure he'd avoid injury, even with the mask.

Bill yelled, "Keep shots on Fat down!"

Armstrong stopped out in front of the blueline. "Why don't you stop me? That's what you're there for."

Jamieson relieved Bill then and while Bill was off Armstrong got the puck again and swept around the defence and in on goal. Fat stayed upright as Armstrong cut in on him. There would have been a good practice play – a shot that would beat most goalies if a man could make it consistently – to try for the small opening on the short side of the net. Armstrong chose to fake. A good goalie would have ignored the fake. But Fat came out and went down and Armstrong's skates barely missed him as he slipped the puck around him and into the goal.

"He's a one-man team," commented one of the brothers, right behind Bill, speaking to one of his friends.

"He's a show-off," Bill said, turning around. He was taut with anger at the danger Fat was in now.

The brother heard. He looked at Bill. Bill stared right back. For the first time in his life an anger was building in him that he had trouble controlling. Red nodded to him and he jumped to the ice as Jamieson came off to rest, and in a few seconds Red dropped the puck and Pete and Pincher were fighting for it as if this game was for the world championship instead of for nothing, just a high school workout. Pete got it, passed to Buchanan, and they were sweeping in. Bill moved slowly backward watchfully so that he could cover both Armstrong and Pete for passes, and Rosy moved at Buchanan, watching him, ready to turn and break for the front of the goal at the pass. But Buchanan didn't pass. Benny Wong hooked the puck away from him with a sweeping check and whirled quickly and sped down the ice, Pincher and Scotty McIntosh rushing to catch up. Warren body-checked Wong. Grouchy got the puck. He passed to Pete, flew in on defence, took the return pass. Bill's body check was a glancing blow. Grouchy was in the clear although a little too far to the right. He cut in to shoot.

Fat went down too fast again. The net was open for a fast flip shot over Fat. But a shot like that might also be dangerous. Fat was scrambling now to his feet. Grouchy took the second best chance and poked the puck along the ice toward an open corner. Fat's flailing legs somehow blocked that shot. Bill tried to slap the rebound away. Pete got it and with a neat bit of stick-handling reached the front of the goal again and tried to shoot between Fat's legs. At the last instant, and undoubtedly by accident, Fat's legs came together and the puck bounced back in front again. Fat dove to try to recover it, dove into the mass of whirling legs and sticks in front of the goal. The puck sat there. Nobody batted at it, because Fat was sprawled on the ice, too close. Then Armstrong dashed in from the side, slapped at the puck, and his stick hit Fat on the side of his head behind the mask. Bill heard the thud of the stick and then the little guy let out a yelp and blood appeared in a gash near his ear.

As Grouchy dropped beside Fat, Bill found himself beside Armstrong and it all happened too fast for him to think. All that he knew was that Fat had been hurt, and two or three players could have slapped at the puck as it lay there, but hadn't. Armstrong had. He grabbed Armstrong by a shoulder and shoved him out of the crowd around Fat, sent him careening several feet away from the goal, and Armstrong, as soon as he recovered, dashed at Bill. All the trouble Armstrong had caused the team so far this year rose in Bill like one solid knot of resentment and his eyes told Armstrong to do his worst, to start something, that he, Bill Spunska, would finish it.

Armstrong demanded, "What was that for?"

With an effort, Bill turned his back and went

in closer to Fat. He was up! That grin was slowly coming back to his face.

"It isn't anything," he was insisting to Red. But a bloody bruise was slowly rising, and Red shot a disgusted look at Armstrong. He resisted temptation to bawl out the kid right there. But he'd seen the byplay between Spunska and Armstrong. Armstrong seemed to have a persecution complex anyway, and the rest of the players were pointedly ignoring him. Red didn't want to increase the tension now. He'd see Armstrong alone later.

"Come on and get some tape on that, Fat," he said.

"And then get back in?" Fat asked.

"Okay, if you're up to it."

"I'm up to it, all right," Fat said. He had no word of reproach for Armstrong. Fat went to the bench for tape, came back, the puck was dropped. And Bill was still mad.

Pete got the puck from Berton this time, passed to Buchanan, went back to his own blue-line to beat the Chief to the puck when Buchanan lost it, and then when he crossed centre ice again Armstrong yelled, coming up fast behind him, and Pete slipped the puck over to that wing. And Bill knew that this was going to be it. He was conscious only of Armstrong's face getting closer and closer and only in the outer ranges of his vision was he conscious of the feinting tactics Armstrong was going through. He could have passed. Bill knew at the last instant, though, that Armstrong had left the pass until too late. He was trying to make a leg-knotted fool out of Spunska again. But he had come too close. With a powerful forward and downward thrust of his shoulders, his stick held low, Bill smacked him, solidly, as hard as he'd ever hit anyone. Everything in him went into that wrenching thud of a check, and Armstrong's feet left the ice and he landed on his own shoulders with a crash; hit, rolled, and lay still.

In a game, Spunska would have been away from there in an instant, following the rest of the play, trying to make an attack click while one of the opposition was still on the ice. But he just stood there, looking down. In a game, play would have gone on among the other players, but they all stopped, too, and crowded around Armstrong, but none very close. It was Fat who came skating out of goal and got down beside Armstrong and lifted his head. Red dashed up. He glanced at Spunska, a quick glance at the boy's suddenly scared face, then started working Armstrong's legs back and forth.

Armstrong moaned and writhed on the ice. His eyes opened.

Then the brothers got there.

One grabbed Spunska by the sweater. "You wood-chopper!" he said, his voice almost a snarl. "They shouldn't let a murderer like you on the ice!"

"That was criminal!" said the other, and grabbed Red Turner and talked away to him.

"You cross-checked him!" the first brother said.

Bill, all anger gone now, feeling empty and spent now that the act of payment was past, was trying to stammer a reply, when Red spoke. He shook off the hands of one brother, pushed past him and wrenched the other away from Spunska. "Shut up, you!" he said. "That was as clean a check as you'll ever see. I saw it. Now you two get off the ice and stay off!"

Armstrong got slowly to his feet. He was pale. He didn't look at Bill. He didn't look at anyone.

"You okay to keep on?" Red asked him. "Better take a rest first. Or quit, if you like."

Armstrong skated slowly toward the boards, his brothers with him, talking. When they reached the gate they all passed through and along the corridor into the dressing room. Bill stood beside Red. He didn't know what to say. He'd wanted to hit Armstrong, but he hadn't wanted to hit him so hard . . . or had he? What had it been that had made him suddenly into a sort of body-check machine over which he had no control? Should he feel ashamed? He didn't. And what would Red say?

But Red avoided his look, skated to centre

and, before there could be any further talk, blew his whistle and dropped the puck. In a minute or two, without Armstrong, the practice was going again.

When the team got to the dressing room at six Armstrong was gone. But Benny Wong had been in to the toilet before he left.

"Said he was okay," Benny told the coach.

"Any cuts or anything?"

Benny shook his head.

Most of the players, eager to get home to eat, dressed and left rapidly. Bill usually was among them. Tonight he hung around. He noticed the silence of the other players. They knew, as he did, that this was serious.

Then he and Fat were the only ones left with the coach, who said heavily, "That was some check, kid."

"I wish I'd saved it for a game," Bill said miserably.

The coach sat down with his back against the wooden wall and tossed his whistle into the air and caught it with a quick nervous motion of his hand. "He's a queer cuss."

Bill said, "I shouldn't have let him get me."

The coach said, "I think I'd better see you two in my office tomorrow noon. Twelve-thirty. Okay?"

"Okay."

CHAPTER 8 ◾

Bill went over that conversation in his mind many times that night in bed. Every time he closed his eyes he could see Armstrong writhing on the ice, the brothers charging in, the argument. . . . Later, in a particularly lucid period just before sleep, he knew that the hot accusations of the minute after the body check made up the memory he really dreaded. In that instant he had been again a new boy, uncertain, unaccepted, and he had done something that made these people call him names. But in the morning this hidden part of his nature was gone with the light and he knew that if there was another practice tonight, and Armstrong acted like that, he'd bash him again.

At the same time, however, he knew that he had met wrong with wrong. If this feud continued it could wreck the team. He thought all morning about the meeting in Mr. Turner's office at noon. What could he do to make things right? He had a gym period before noon. When he was showering, he thought of Sarah. She knew Armstrong in a better way than most people, as a friend. The *Life with Father* cast met almost every noon in the auditorium to go over a few scenes. Because of the meeting in the coach's office later, Armstrong wouldn't be there, probably. He hoped not anyway.

Bill got to the auditorium shortly after the noon bell. The auditorium was one of the brightest places in a bright, airy school. One wall was all glass brick. The group around the stage turned quickly as he came in. Armstrong wasn't among them.

They were eating their lunches and chatting. Bill walked down and sat by Sarah.

Her voice had an edge. "Come to carry on the argument? He isn't here."

"I was going to see if you knew how we could stop arguing."

The others had been curious for a minute but now had taken up their conversation again.

"You know him better than I do, Sarah."

Sarah was eating a butter tart. Bill was hungry. The sight of her lunch made him think of his own. She must have seen that. She had another butter tart. She offered it to him.

"You need it," he said.

"Eat it!"

He did.

"He's always all right with us," Sarah said.

"At first I thought that the team must be picking on him, to make him act that way. Pete said you weren't. But he also said that you seemed to have a lower boiling point with him than the rest of the team."

Bill shrugged. He hadn't thought of it quite that way before, but it was true, he guessed. The others must have been mad. But they had held off. He hadn't.

"I've thought about it a lot," she said. "Naturally. Remember how Pete was last year when we had to transfer from Daniel Mac? Everybody resented him for a while, and he returned the compliment. He'd been a big man at Daniel Mac and he had to start all over again at Northwest. Well, Armstrong is like Pete, it seems to me."

"Except that Pete made the adjustment," Bill said.

"If you and the others had made Cliff feel like a big shot at Northwest, too, I think everything would have been different."

"But we never make each other feel like big shots! Why should he be different? But maybe you're right! Maybe if we had handled it better, appointed a committee, or something, to butter up Armstrong . . ."

Sarah laughed at his tone. "There you go again."

"I guess so."

He looked at the clock on the wall and found he had only ten minutes to eat and get to the coach's office. Sarah hadn't really helped him. They weren't going to butter up Armstrong. Why should they?

At twelve-thirty Red glanced up from his desk at Bill in the doorway and called, "I guess we'll have to postpone this. Armstrong isn't at school today."

As Bill came in, looking baffled, Red was going over in his mind what his course should be now. If Armstrong had been here, they could have threshed it out, aired it, maybe laid the basis for some kind of peace. But since Armstrong hadn't turned up at school he didn't know what to think. Maybe it would be better to go back to the course he'd been following until that fracas in practice. He'd been frankly just letting Armstrong's attitude slide, hoping that it would adjust itself, that somehow the good feeling of team and comradeship would catch up Armstrong and straighten him out. It had seemed all right to do it that way. After all, he'd played well. Now he wondered about the game tomorrow night. If we can get through it without another blow-up – and we should; it isn't as if Armstrong and Spunska will be playing *against* one another – there'll be ten days of Christmas holiday for them to cool off and see the light. The truth was that Red was reluctant to arbitrate an affair that really concerned something deep down in both boys, something that could be corrected completely only by their own efforts, not by a coach's knocking their heads together and telling them to smarten up.

He made up his mind. He wasn't a man who made a habit of putting off important things, but he also knew that some things were better put off. Maybe it was just as well Armstrong had stayed home from school today. Maybe this meeting, bringing up all the issues, would just have widened the breach. "Just let it slide for now, Bill."

Armstrong was missing from school again Friday. At noon Fat said that the coach, making up the lineup, had phoned his home. Armstrong had said he'd be okay for the Gordon Bell game tonight, so he was on the lineup.

Fat had more news. "And guess who's the spare goalie!" At the groan that went up around the lunch table, he only grinned. "Coach said I did pretty well in there!" he said. "And so I did, too! But just to cheer you guys up, he's called for volunteers to come out to the next practice."

"Brabant!" said Rosy piously. "May the saints preserve you and make you a man of iron."

That night in the dressing room, Armstrong acted exactly as if there had been no incident in practice. He and Mitch and a few others chatted away as usual.

The score was tied 1-1 in the second period, a goal by Pincher Martin matched by one by Jones, when the blow-up came.

The Gordon line was on, with Spunska and Rosy on defense. Armstrong was going well. Pete was feeding him pass after pass, but the goalie kicked out shot after shot. Some of the saves seemed like miracles. Then Forsyth of Gordon Bell led a rush down centre ice, wingers forming up with him. He held his pass too late. Rosy hit him. The puck skidded over to Bill, and he was away.

His rushes always pulled the crowd to its feet. He plunged straight down centre ice – his clumsiness adding colour to the rush – gaining speed as he neared the Gordon Bell blueline. Because of the confusion following the last play nobody was in position for a pass. Armstrong was turning on right wing, Buchanan on left, and Pete had been knocked down. Bill went in alone, around a defenceman, right to the goalmouth. He blasted a shot at an open side. The goalie batted it out. Bill slapped at the loose puck back-handed, trying to knock it in, but missed the puck altogether. In doing so, he went off balance. As he fell, his stick hit the Gordon Bell goalie and knocked him to one side of the net. Bill sprawled there, trying to get up. He was out of the goal crease, but his stick was tangled with the Gordon Bell goalie. Armstrong dashed in and slapped the puck into the net.

Armstrong jumped in the air as the red light went on. Some others who hadn't seen the play closely yelled at him in elation. Then the referee, Dick Dunsford, rushed in blowing his whistle and waving his hands flat out, palms down, to signal no goal. Bill had just got to his feet when Dunsford tapped his shoulder and said, "Two minutes in the cooler, kid."

The swiftness of the play had been too much.

"Why?" Bill yelled.

"Interfering with the goalkeeper."

Then Armstrong, at centre ice, suddenly realized that the goal he had celebrated so vociferously had been disallowed. He rushed at Dunsford. Northwest and Gordon Bell players gathered in fast-talking knots, arguing the point among themselves.

Bill had an urge to bang his stick on the ice in disgust. He didn't. He didn't want to get a misconduct as well as the minor penalty. He was mad, but he had been in the wrong and he knew it. He was about to skate to the penalty box when Armstrong turned from Dunsford, who wouldn't argue with anybody but a team captain or alternate, and stormed after him.

He grabbed Bill by the shoulder and twisted him around. His face was red with anger. "Get in there, Spunska," he said. "That's what you're supposed to be alternate captain for! Get in there and tell that fool off!"

Dunsford heard the last part of that. "Cool off, Armstrong," he said. "Or you won't be playing any more tonight."

"Argue!" Armstrong yelled at Bill.

"I was interfering," Bill said. "I'm sorry. But that makes it no goal."

Dunsford said, "I'm certainly glad to meet an honest man once in a while in this racket." Armstrong suddenly quieted. But his was a quiet full of another kind of anger.

"Okay," he said. "I get it." And he skated away.

"What the heck's the matter with that guy?" Dunsford said. Then he blew his whistle. "Get moving, Spunska. . . ."

Bill skated toward the penalty box. Dunsford faced off to start play again. Red sent Grouchy out to defence with Warren and pulled off the Gordon line and put Berton and Big Canoe on to try to kill off the penalty for the two minutes Northwest would be short-handed.

They did kill off that penalty, the Chief ragging the puck in centre ice once for a full minute, dodging and skating with it to keep it from Gordon Bell. Bill got back on the ice just at the end of the period.

When he got into the dressing room he was

walking past the rubbing table to the bucket full of halved oranges when Armstrong said, "If that had been Pete Gordon scored that goal, or anybody else but me, you'd all be arguing until kingdom come that it was a good goal."

Bill said, "If it's illegal, it's illegal, that's all there is to it. Works both ways. It'll work for us, sometime."

The rest of the dressing room was quiet. Red lifted one hand as if to interfere, even opened his mouth, then was silent. The snowball was rolling. It couldn't be stopped. He could only hope it would get to the bottom safely. Some did.

Armstrong sat down. "Everybody's right but Armstrong," he said.

DeGruchy glanced at Red. Red merely shrugged. Grouchy knew he wasn't going to interfere yet. So he got into it.

"The thing is, Cliff," he said, "the referee was right. I can't figure out you wanting Bill to argue for you when you know darn well we're in the wrong."

Armstrong jumped up. He had been quiet before. Now he wasn't. "I *don't* know!" he said. "Only Spunska knows!"

The inference was clear, that Bill might not even have been honest in admitting he was interfering with the goalie. Bill lost control. He sprang at Armstrong. Grouchy jumped in and held them apart. Then as quickly as he had lost his temper, Bill regained it. He felt physically sick.

Red had to get into it now. His voice wasn't tough, but it was firm. It was time to end this. "Cliff, you've accused Spunska of a mean kind of dishonesty. I saw the play. Spunska was interfering with the goalie. In my opinion, I don't think he could move fast enough to get out of there before the goal was scored. I don't think Spunska would hurt the team just to spite you. I think you should take that back."

Armstrong hesitated, then shrugged and turned away. Red's voice suddenly got cool and hard.

"Maybe let's put it this way," Red said. "Either you admit that maybe you were wrong or you'd better sit out the rest of this game and think things over a little." He was thinking, if the team is going to be blown wide open by this kind of argument, let's have it now, in the middle of the season, so we can get it patched up before the playoffs. "What do you say?"

"I'm not going to apologize," Armstrong said.

"Take off your sweater then," Red said curtly.

Bill could scarcely bear to watch or listen. It was as if a thing he loved was being broken before his eyes. And right or wrong, a lot was his fault.

112

"We're due on the ice," Red said. "Let's go."

The team rose and walked quickly but without words or spirit toward the door. Mitchell hesitated just long enough so that Red noticed it and knew Mitchell was with Armstrong in this argument, at least part way.

At the door, Red turned. One more chance. No more. "If you want to come up any time in the next five minutes, after you think this over, you'll be welcome, Cliff," Red said. "If you can't make up your mind in that time, get dressed and go home. What I say goes for just this game. We can talk over the long-term aspects of it on Monday."

He closed the door behind him. He was glad the corridor was empty. He didn't want to meet anyone who would ask him any questions just yet. As he mounted the steps a vagrant hope came to him that Armstrong would come up. Surely he had more sense than to quit on this team. The thing Red couldn't shake out of his mind, though, was the fact that Mitchell almost had stayed with Armstrong. Red searched back through games and practices. Had Armstrong really been treated badly? He could find nothing that the boy hadn't brought on himself. As his feet reached the ice and the cheers and boos and cries of "Let's get going!" greeted his tardy appearance, he saw Cliff's brothers. He thought, rather angrily, there's a lot of the trouble. They're always pushing him, hard. Even the best kid can't stand that.

The game started. Busy making changes in his lineup to cope with the loss of Armstrong, Red hardly had time to think for the next few minutes. He moved Rosy up to Armstrong's wing, began to alternate the three remaining defencemen. Then the five-minute deadline was gone. Armstrong hadn't appeared. Lee Vincent slipped down from the press box and kneeled by Red so as not to obstruct the view of people behind. "What happened?" he asked.

"It broke," Red said. "It's bad."

"I'll see you later," Lee said.

"Okay."

In all the conjecture in the crowd about why Armstrong hadn't come out for the third period, it was almost an anticlimax that Bush got a goal on a long shot early in the period and Northwest fought back hard until Pete Gordon tied it on a pass from Spunska with less than two minutes to play, so the game finished in a 2-2 draw. In the intermission between that game and the one between Kelvin and Daniel Mac, which ended eventually in a scoreless tie, all the talk in the lobby was on the flying rumours that the dissension in Northwest's team finally had split it wide open.

CHAPTER 9 ◼

When the last player was in the dressing room after the game, Red lingered at the door. Lee Vincent came along with the referee and the timer. The referee looked curiously at the Northwest coach as they passed. Lee stopped.

"Look, Lee," Red said. "I'll see you after the kids have dressed. Would you stay here at the door and keep everybody out? Don't even let 'em knock. I've got something to say."

"Sure."

Red closed the door and locked it on the inside and paced up and down the dressing room floor as his players undressed. Amazing how the absence of one man could leave such a hole. The dressing room benches, piled as they were with equipment, looked half bare. And the kids did nothing to liven it up, naturally. They were badly shaken. Some started to undress. Some just sat. Red caught their eyes following him, waiting for him to speak.

Finally, he wheeled, his hands shoved deeply into his pockets. "A lot of people will be asking you a lot of questions," he said. "I'm not going to tell you what to say. But remember this – we're in a spot. We're going to try to get this team back together again if we can. Don't say anything that will make the patch-up job harder. That's all for now."

He unlocked the door and went out. As the door opened, Bill saw that Mr. Anderson, the Northwest principal, was waiting there with Lee Vincent. News got around fast. Red spoke to both of them as he went out and closed the door.

There had been practically no talking until then. Rosy was the first to break it. "It's a good riddance," he said.

Mitchell flared up. "You're crazy!"

"Can't lose our top scorer and call it a good thing," Grouchy said.

"He didn't do us good," Rosy said stubbornly.

Warren, who'd had very little to say about this inner battle since it began, although Armstrong had tried hard to recruit him, now said, "There must be some way we can get him back. He was half our team out there tonight before that business about the goal."

Bill said to Grouchy, suddenly, "Could I have done anything, Grouchy?"

"Nothing but what you did. But that doesn't make it a good thing."

Pete was dressing beside Bill. "We were going

to have this blow-up anyway," he said quietly. "Better to have it now than in the playoffs."

"If we make the playoffs," Grouchy said.

"Heck," Pincher Martin said, "we're leading the league! We'd have to fall flat on our faces to miss the playoffs now."

Grouchy said, "This isn't the same team we had for the last four games."

Bill caught the undertone of meaning. The loss of Armstrong was one thing, and serious enough. But this anger of Alec Mitchell with the rest of the club was an additional problem. Mitch wasn't a star, but he was one of the team's best checkers, a steady winger on Hurry Berton's line. If Armstrong was suspended for keeps, and Mitch slackened up, the team could easily lose that hairbreadth edge which makes the difference between winning and losing.

"Want a lift home?" Pete asked Bill. "I've got the car."

"Thanks."

Sarah was waiting for them. The three of them left the rink together, out to the icy streets. For a while nobody spoke, then Sarah said, "How serious is all this?"

"I don't know," Bill said, remembering that earlier tonight he'd thought there'd be a chance soon to bury the hatchet with Armstrong. They'd certainly strayed a long way from that.

Pete answered her, too. "It doesn't have to be

serious, if Armstrong cools off and comes back."

"That's a big 'if,' " Bill said heavily.

"Look," Pete said. "It just happened. We won't know how serious it is for days anyway. Let's just let it ride."

Bill tried to let it ride. But he had to explain it to his mother and father. And they found it hard to understand, he could see.

He tried to let it ride the next day at work, too, but he couldn't. The papers were full of it. The radio sportscasts, including the one on the warehouse radio just as work started that morning, were full of it. One sportscaster said, "It won't be the first good team ruined by dissension, or the last."

When Armstrong didn't turn up at school on Monday there was an immediate rumour throughout the school that he had quit Northwest. But the principal cleared that up quickly. On Friday, Armstrong had phoned to ask permission to miss school Monday and Tuesday, the last two days before Christmas holidays. One of his brothers had to go East on business and Cliff was going along. "He said something about going to a couple of National Hockey League games," Mr. Anderson told Red in the teachers' room that noon. "And since he's well up in his work, I told him he could go. They flew, I believe, because Cliff also said something about being back at his home in Brandon in time for Christmas."

"How do you get along with Armstrong?" Red asked one of Armstrong's teachers.

The teacher said, "Well, he's been a good student. But he has seemed rather preoccupied lately. This Spunska boy seems to have riled him pretty badly, though, eh?"

"I hope to patch that up," Red said.

Later that day Bill called in at the sports office. He wanted to ask if there was anything new. Red took one look at his face and then spoke with more confidence than he felt. "Cheer up, kid," he said. "I think we'll be all right. One big thing in our favour is that Armstrong would rather play hockey than eat. And he also has ambitions to be a pro. He'll know that he can't get to be a pro by sitting at home sulking while other boys strut their stuff for the scouts."

Bill had often read about people who lost themselves in their work. He'd never quite known what it meant until he got caught up in the Christmas rush around Desmond's. It had been gathering momentum for a week, but in the last two days before Christmas it seemed that all at once every tobacco shop and corner store in the city had sold out all their Christmas-wrapped cigars, cigarettes, tobaccos, and chocolates, and wanted more. He worked three hours overtime on Tuesday, the last day of school, and when he left at nine Albert asked him to be in the next day at seven, an hour early.

That final day before Christmas, Desmond's was a madhouse. It seemed to Bill that he carried tons. He'd plunk one armload on the wrapping table, tie it, shove the invoice under the string, grab another invoice, and hurry away to fill the next order. He began to worry about the presents he still hadn't bought. Dad was no problem. He loved cigars. With his employee discount, he could get Dad a box of twenty-five good cigars for ten dollars. That would leave Mother. But what to get her? He didn't want to be rushing around hunting, but he couldn't think of anything. Rather, he could think of lots of things, but all cost more than he had. He watched the clock, hoping the last thick tide of orders would thin out soon.

They did, about noon. Where all had been activity, rushing, half an hour before, suddenly the whole city seemed to be relaxing for Christmas. Albert's quick marches around the warehouse never had slowed until now, when he filled the last order himself and then came back and sank into his chair. "Feet," he said, "I'm sorry. Truly I am."

Herbie was sitting on the wrapping table lighting a cigarette. The drivers came in, picked up the last few orders, and said they'd be back in a few minutes. The place was closing at two today. Bill got a Coke from the case in the corner and dropped his money for it in the old tobacco tin there. He intended to stand up and drink it and then run. But his legs just wouldn't let him. He sat down. Nobody spoke. The three of them watched the waning activity in the front office. The last invoices were filed. The last phones were closed off. The computer screen went dark.

"This is a tough enough game, too, eh, Bill?" Albert asked.

"Has been the last few days."

"You've sure earned your keep, boy," Albert said.

Bill stretched and was about to go for his coat when he saw Mr. McClelland come out of his office. He said something that brought smiles and replies from the office staff – the phone girls, cashier, bookkeeper, the four city salesmen, the credit manager. Bill was moving slowly toward the coatrack.

"Wait a minute," Albert said.

Bill waited, wondering what was up.

The people from the office filed out into the warehouse. Mr. McClelland broke out a new case of Cokes and handed them around. There was an odd formal constraint about this which didn't go with the rush of the last few days, nor with the shelves of stock, the oiled wooden floor, the working air of the place. The drivers piled through the back door and walked down the ramp self-consciously – the first time Bill ever had seen them other than wisecracking and assured.

They were all there now, fifteen of them, everyone who worked for John Desmond, Ltd. Mr. McClelland stood up, looking around.

"Not going to make a speech," he said. "Not much of one, anyway. You guys and girls all worked just about twice as hard as you get paid for these last few days. I know most of you would rather have a firm handshake and a clap on the back than money, any time – " a chuckle went around the warehouse at that – "but nevertheless we're going to try to force an extra week's pay on each of you."

There was a quick burst of appreciation. Eyes lighted up. People turned to one another and smiled. "Amazing how the mention of money perks people up," Albert said loudly, and they all laughed. Bill's first quick excitement abated. He'd only worked here a month. Would he be counted in? Must be, or Albert wouldn't have told him to wait. But would he get a whole week's pay? He couldn't believe that. . . . But anything would help. He thought of a dozen things he could buy for Mother for Christmas if he just had a little more money.

He didn't have long to wait. Mr. McClelland was calling out the names, handing out the bonus envelopes. With each, he made some little comment. To Herbie, he said, "For the only man I know who can do a hundred yards in ten seconds and finish with an armful of cigarettes." Albert he called "the only man who thinks that when the army told him to march, it meant forever." And when he only had one envelope left in his hand Bill knew that he was going to get one. Mr. McClelland was saying, "Bill Spunska, come up here."

Bill felt the warmth in the way some of the people he passed spoke to him. When he got in front of Mr. McClelland the boss handed him the envelope and said, "It didn't take you long to fit in, boy. You're welcome as long as you want to stay. . . . Okay! No more talk. Merry Christmas, everybody!"

They all said Merry Christmas in return to him, and in a few minutes Bill was out in front, calling Merry Christmas to the others. He hadn't wanted to open the envelope while anyone was watching. He walked along the street, then stopped to open it. Inside was one bill, a fifty. He walked a block without remembering anything, his feet hardly touching the ground. Fifty extra dollars! Then he slowed. An argument developed in his mind. If he gave the whole thing to Dad they'd be that much farther ahead with the national debt. That was the thing to do. Now, to find something for Mother. He was passing a jewelry store. He looked in the window. Then he went in. He saw it immediately, an exquisite vase, big, a deep burnished red, a fine glowing red. . . . It would be too expensive, of course. He looked at the tag. $51.95. Marked down from $80. But heck, he'd be crazy! No, couldn't buy that. Yet it was beautiful, really beautiful.

A clerk said, "Can I do anything for you?"

"Yes," Bill said, "I'd like this vase, please."

It was a total abandonment of years of austerity – years that stretched back as far as he could remember. Snow began to fall, falling on his face as he walked rapidly southward toward home, carrying his presents.

CHAPTER 10 ▬

For as long as he could remember, Bill had been daydreaming of one kind of Christmas. On that Christmas in his daydreams he'd be like the other boys he knew. He'd get out of bed early in the morning while it was still dark. He'd know that it was too early to get up, but he'd creep downstairs anyway and look at the softly lighted Christmas tree from the stairs, trying to figure out which of the many big parcels were for him. And then his parents would get up and they would come down together and open wonderful presents, big ones, expensive ones; and later at breakfast, the first subtle smells of the huge turkey cooking for dinner would begin to permeate the house and the day would go on and on and on. . . .

But his Christmases until now had been different. He could hardly remember the last one in Poland. The Christmases in England had been as good as Mother could make them, but they had been sad rather than happy, wondering what Dad was doing, when he could join them. If ever. And in one room, with a hot plate for cooking, there'd been no place to cook a real dinner. Last year, for what might have been the first real Christmas, Mother had been sick. They'd had the Christmas tree in her room and dinner had been on plates on their knees as they sat there with her.

Bill thought those thoughts on Christmas morning as he waked and got up and looked from his window at the fading stars above the quiet frosty world. This, in a way, was the first Christmas for the Spunskas. The bare painted wooden floor was cold on his feet, so he pulled on his dressing gown and socks. He made no noise leaving his room. But there was a light on, downstairs! He went a little faster. The stairs creaked. Then he saw that the Christmas tree was lighted – lights he'd never seen before. They must have waited until he was in bed before stringing them – and then left them on. Had they guessed that dream of his? He crouched a little so he could look through the archway into the living room at the presents under the tree, and he heard no whisper from above, no noise at all. But suddenly there was a shout, "Merry Christmas!" A light snapped on. Dad and Mother were standing at the top of the stairs, looking down on him, coming down.

Then they were both beside him, each with

an arm around him, and the Spunskas went down the rest of the way together.

They gathered around the tree, the early light creeping in, the house warming, the lights of the tree making a glow warmer than daylight in the corner where Bill took presents from the tree and passed them around. There was a catch in his throat at the look on Mother's face when she saw the vase. She held it up to the light and looked at it and didn't say anything at all for a minute; and Bill was thinking that it was amazing to be able to exchange such ordinary stuff as money for the soft inner glow of the vase and the look of astonishment and pleasure on his dad's face and the indescribable look of his mother, the look she always had for a thing of beauty, as care and years fell away from her face and left her expression as pure and smooth and happy as if nothing existed in the world but this beautiful vase and herself. She came over and kissed him, hugging his shoulders hard.

Then came the cigars for Dad. A book for Dad, from Mother. A bed jacket for Mother, from Dad. And then Bill unwrapped the big box that was for him, and opened the lid, and on top was a new book, a biography of Lech Walesa, and underneath in the white tissue paper was his big present, a new coat.

He jumped up, holding it out before him. "Boy!" he said.

"Like it?" Dad asked.

"Like it!" Bill replied. "I sure do!"

They watched, pretending to be critical, as he tried it on. He had never mentioned about that old coat of his, the trench coat brought from England, how cold it was. But they had known. He'd been going to save after Christmas to buy himself a new one. Now he didn't have to. He knew half a dozen boys in school who had coats exactly like this, belted three-quarter-length dark blue wool with a thick quilted wool lining and a big fur collar. It was good that it was like others worn to school. Those boys were well dressed. Now he was, too.

It was the Christmas of his dreams, exactly, even to the first subtle smells of the turkey just as they were finishing their breakfast. It had been all ready, stuffed and trussed, and Mother had put it in the oven first thing, dashing out to do it while the others were still standing before the untouched tree.

Bill could hardly wait to wear his coat. He had to go out, just to wear it. So after breakfast he went out to call on the Gordons. At noon he was back home again. The smell of the turkey was all through the house now, upstairs and down. For a couple of hours Bill spent most of his time in the warm and fragrant kitchen watching Mother put the finishing touches on a meal that they began eating at two and finished at three-thirty in such a drowsy state of well-being that Bill could scarcely get to his feet to leave the table. From then on the day lived up to the high promise of its beginning. Some people from the university dropped in. Mother and Dad visited the neighbours. Grouchy came in. Pincher Martin dropped by, with Fat Abramson. It was nine when the last callers left and the Spunskas sat around their kitchen table and had turkey sandwiches thick with cranberry, made on fresh bread Mother had put into the oven when the turkey came out.

In bed he read his new book, felt in his mind again the good feel of his new coat, ate the meat from a turkey drumstick, ate an apple, then slept.

CHAPTER 11 ◄

Ever since Bill had asked Sarah out, weeks ago,
and she already had promised she'd go out with
Armstrong, he'd been thinking about asking
her again. He'd decide to do it the next time he
got to a phone. Then he'd get to the phone and
change his mind. He knew why, and it bothered
him. He'd get thinking about what a good time
they'd have; and then he'd think, what if she
can't come? What if she says "No" again?

That lasted until a few days after Christmas.
Bill got home one evening from a couple of
hours of mainly loafing at Desmond's – where
the Christmas rush had now given way to the
after-Christmas doldrums – and Dad pulled an
envelope from his pocket and tossed it over to
him.

"What's this?" Bill asked, opening it.

"Two tickets to opening night of the Winnipeg Players."

The Winnipeg Players were a stock company
which would open for the season on New Year's
Eve.

"Aren't you going?" Bill asked.

"We're going to a party that night," Mother said. "The wife of the head of your father's department phoned a few days ago. You remember . . ."

Bill was looking at the tickets. The show was called *The Ghost Train*. Sounded good.

"Whom will you ask?" Mother said. "Sarah?"

Bill laughed. "You're reading my mind."

On the way over to the Gordons that night he was sure she would say "No." It was too late. It was only four days until New Year's. She'd be going out with someone else. But who else? Because he was so friendly with Pete, he knew pretty well whom she saw. There was no one else he knew of except Armstrong. And he was away.

Finally he went into a drugstore and phoned. It would be easier taking defeat over the phone than face to face.

He told her he had these tickets and asked if she would come.

She said, "I'd love to!"

It seemed very simple, after it was all over.

At quarter to seven on New Year's Eve Bill trotted upstairs to get ready for the date. He'd got home at six-thirty, eaten a little, lost his appetite, and tried to ignore the amused glances of his parents as he excused himself and left the table. He ran a hot bath, got in, thought he'd soap himself and then soak. He soaped himself, lay down, sloshed water around to remove the soap, got up quickly, and was half dried before he remembered that he'd been going to soak. Just in time he remembered to use the last of the water to clean the bathtub. Should he shave? Heck, he'd only shaved yesterday. Or was it the day before? He shaved, cleaned his teeth, washed his hair, combed it still wet so it would stay in place when it dried (or froze, he thought), and called downstairs, "What time is it?"

"Five to seven," Dad called back.

All that in ten minutes?

In his room he looked at his good shoes. They gleamed – he hadn't worn them since the last time he polished them. He went downstairs to fetch an old piece of newspaper and came back up and spread it on the floor so he wouldn't get polish all over, and polished them again. There was polish on his hands. So he went back in the bathroom and washed again. Then he came back, put on clean underwear, socks, white shirt, shoes, and slacks. He tried a Windsor knot in his tie. He didn't like it with this shirt. He tied an ordinary knot. Then he put on his jacket.

Was the tie too red?

He went to the top of the stairs and called down, "What time is it now?"

Dad called back solemnly, "Five past seven."

All the time he knew this was crazy. It wasn't as if he'd never been out with a girl before. But the other times, you know – hockey games, school dances, there were always other people around. Crowds of them. People he knew. This was different. This was Sarah he'd be sitting alone with, even in a crowd – maybe holding hands, like they had sometimes before. The few times he and Sarah had kissed had made him feel like he never had before. Now that he had a little money maybe they could do more things together . . .

He finally made it to the living room and stood undecided in the archway.

His parents looked up. "You look fine," Dad said.

"Very handsome," Mother said.

"What time is it?" Bill asked.

"Quarter past seven."

He couldn't sit still. Five minutes later, after staring at the paper for a while without seeing any of the words, he got up and put on his new coat.

It fitted perfectly, looked terrific.

"Better go," Dad said, "before you blow up."

On the way downtown in the bus, Bill was proud of the way Sarah looked. She wore on her hair a filmy black thing that sparkled. She seemed excited, too. He wondered if she felt the same way he did. She couldn't, of course. Quite often when he glanced at her, she glanced at him too. A funny feeling.

In the crowd around the entrance to the theatre Bill suddenly felt that everything he had on was wrong. His hands seemed too big. He met no one's eye. For a frantic moment he thought he'd forgotten the tickets, although he had put his hand on them at least a dozen times during the walk to Sarah's and the ride downtown. He got them out, gave them to a man, and they went in.

It was only when they got to their seats and saw that few of the others had coats with them that he remembered what he'd forgotten.

"I forgot to check the coats," he said, much daunted.

Sarah said, as if it were nothing, "We'll hold them on our knees."

They sat awhile, watching the theatre fill up, and gradually, as they talked casually about people who came in, read their programs, and looked around, Bill began to relax. Many people were looking at them. But now he knew that it was because of Sarah. She was the best-looking girl here. He was lucky.

And just before the curtain went up their elbows happened to touch, and he looked at her and she looked at him.

"This is fun, eh?" he said, then amended hastily, "For me, anyway."

"It's fun for me, too. Especially . . ."

"Especially what?"

"You seem to know exactly what you're doing all the time. You don't get flustered. It must be that Continental poise. . . ." Her voice was light, slightly mocking, but she was serious.

He laughed. People looked at him, smiled at his laughter, but it didn't matter now.

"Why are you laughing?" she asked.

"If that's the way I seemed," he said, "I should be in this play, instead of sitting out here."

The lights went down and the curtain up. They watched. They laughed, applauded, lost in the illusion of the stage.

It was a good evening. They talked on the way home on the bus in a way that wouldn't have been possible only a few hours ago. They talked frankly about Armstrong, for one thing.

He started it by asking if she'd heard from him.

"No," she said.

"I thought you would." He was kidding her a little.

"So did I," she said. "He missed the last rehearsal, you know."

"When are you putting on the play?"

"The end of January." She was quiet a few seconds, then said, "What about him and the hockey team?"

"No change." Bill said. "But the next time I see him I'm going to suggest that he and I start over again." He had thought of this a lot in the last week, when there was no hockey, no Armstrong, no school. He thought he had the right perspective now. "I don't see why we can't go right on not liking each other particularly, but agree not to let it interfere with the team."

"So do I."

They walked up the freshly swept walk to the Gordons' veranda. It was nearly midnight.

"Come on in for a while," she said. "Pete's having a bridge game, I think. And we can watch TV and hear the New Year bells and whistles and all that stuff."

"Okay. Thanks."

When Sarah and Bill walked into the living room, Pete and Pincher Martin and Winston Kryschuk and Stretch Buchanan were playing bridge, with the TV blaring at them. Pete was playing a hand. They looked up, Pete absently, the others smiling and calling greetings. The Christmas decorations were still up and the room had a warm and festive air. The bridge players were intent as Pete played his third last card, yipped cheerfully when a king fell, and took the rest.

"Four spades," he said. "Doubled. Quick rubber."

"Lucky!" Pincher said. "Boy, you were hung with luck!"

"Must be some bridge game," Sarah said, "with all that noise from the TV."

"Didn't want to miss the midnight celebration," Pete said, pushing back his chair. "And that station gives sports news – I guess even on New Year's Eve. Like to know how Kelvin made out in that exhibition they played tonight in Brandon."

The bridge game apparently was over. Sarah got Cokes and some little mince tarts from the kitchen, and the six of them sat around and talked. Bill was dressed much more formally than the others and felt slightly embarrassed by it. He'd felt good about it when he was out with Sarah, but this atmosphere was different.

The announcer yelled, "Happy New Year!"

The six of them got up and joined hands and danced around, singing "Auld Lang Syne" with the television. Then they collapsed into chairs, laughing and quieting gradually, and later listened through a newscast until the announcer said, "And now for the sports. Not much tonight. Most leagues leave this night blank and let the players celebrate like other people, for a change. But there is an interesting item here from Brandon. Tonight the Brandon Collegiate team beat Kelvin, 3-2, in an exhibition game played in the Wheat City. Kelvin led 2-1 going into the third period. Brandon's tying and winning goals were scored by Cliff Armstrong, who played the first part of the season with Northwest. . . ."

The room was absolutely quiet with shock as the announcer went on.

". . . The story from Brandon says that Armstrong has returned there to live and will line up for the rest of the season with the team on which he starred last year."

CHAPTER 12 ■

The yells that greeted Northwest's appearance on the ice against St. John's Tech two nights later weren't by any means all cheers. In the first game, with Kelvin beating Daniel Mac 3-1 to draw to within one point of Northwest, the crowd had been almost quiet, as if saving its breath for Northwest.

"Yah, hot-shots!" one boy yelled. "Where's your big man?"

"Did Army-marmy get maddy-waddy?" yelled a high falsetto.

"Hey, four eyes!" shouted a boy with a deep voice. "Come out from behind those goggles!" That was for Jamieson, who, when taping his spectacles to his temples in the dressing room earlier, had said it made him feel like a space-man. Rosy had moved up to right wing on Pete's line, so Jamieson was back in the lineup.

"Spunska!" a girl called, as he came close to the boards once. "Now that you got rid of him are you going to score all Armstrong's goals?" Some of these jabs were from the Northwest section.

Even without this riding they got from the crowd, the team had gone to the ice shaken. All day long, this first day back at school, the corridors at Northwest had hummed with ceaseless talk about the rights and wrongs of Armstrong's decision to go back to Brandon. By game time tonight Bill wished he'd never heard the name Cliff Armstrong. Everyone, at school, at work, neighbours along the street, wanted to talk about Armstrong. What kind of a guy is he, anyway? Why'd he go back to Brandon? Say, maybe you guys will play him in the provincial final now! Is it true you beat him up three or four times? I heard that nobody on the Northwest team ever spoke to Armstrong from the minute he showed at a practice, is that right?

Now they played like sleepwalkers. Pete's line, with Rosy on the right wing, looked pitiful. Bill made mistake after mistake. Grouchy tried valiantly to get the team playing effectively, but it was no use. The team operated like a machine that had broken down and been patched with hairpins and baling wire. It ran, all right, but neither smoothly nor well. St. John's led 4-0 by the time Grouchy scored the only Northwest goal late in the third period. Northwest went to its dressing room at the end of the game beaten for the first time this season.

The talk had been bad enough before. Now, with that humbling by a team that had won only one of its first four games, it got worse. A lot of it was ridiculous, but some of it wasn't, and by now Bill knew he was in for a rough time. He ran a constant gauntlet of questioning in the halls. He could find no defence. It seemed to him that to the average student the team wasn't made up of people at all. To them it was sort of a goal-scoring machine which they had believed guaranteed against breakdown, or even slowdown. Some of the kids he knew told him he'd done right, all right, *but* . . . There was always that *but*. Bill knew that it stood for, *But nothing should be allowed to wreck the hockey team*. The trouble was, he agreed. He blamed himself. He had let the side down by tangling openly with Armstrong. Red had handled him strongly but without incident. Grouchy had been firm without being antagonistic. The straight fact was that he, Bill Spunska, had refused to let Armstrong's hockey ability be separated from his unpleasant personality. And by tangling with one, he had lost the other for the team. And now, what could he do about it? There seemed no answer.

There was one angle of the Armstrong retreat that he hadn't thought of, though. One morning he passed Sarah in the hall. He was rushing to get to their room. She reached out and held his arm.

"All right," she said, "slow down, boy. You've

been going around looking like the breath of death long enough."

No one can be more indignant than someone accused of excessive self-pity. Bill was huffy. "I've got reasons."

"Reasons, smeasons!" she said. "Now you take me, I've really got troubles."

"What?"

"How would you like to be the Mama in *Life with Father*, with no Father?"

"Gosh," Bill said. "The dramatic society!" For some reason or other, at that point, the thought that Armstrong had run out on the dramatic society struck him as being funny.

"Don't you laugh!" Sarah said.

"How about his understudy?"

"We had trouble finding anyone at all to play the part, let alone an understudy!"

"What are you going to do?"

"We'll find someone. But we haven't yet. And we're supposed to put on the play at the end of the month." She paused. "He wrote me a letter," she said, with a slight self-consciousness.

He stopped abruptly in the doorway of the room. "What did he say, or is that any of my business?"

She shoved Bill gently into the room so they wouldn't block the doorway. "Oh, that he hated to let us down, that he'd done a lot of thinking about it and just decided it was the only thing for him to do – all that stuff. He said one funny thing. . . ."

"What?"

"That he'd feel better about playing in Brandon again, where the heat wasn't on him all the time. . . . I think he'd figured out that his brothers were pushing him into things."

"His brothers didn't push him into the dramatic society, though," Bill said.

"No needling!"

They stood by a window. Bill could tell from Sarah's manner, rather than her light words, that she was upset about Armstrong's gumming up their play as much as he had gummed up the hockey team. In a way, it had been an easy out for Armstrong, just pulling out in the face of trouble. In another way, it had been a hard out. He had left behind a lot of people who wouldn't trust him again. Bill couldn't help feeling glad that Sarah was one of them. But the more he thought about it, the less he was inclined really to blame Armstrong. It must have been rough here: not liked, goaded by his brothers, missing the cheers he'd got as Brandon's big man. Bill grinned to himself wryly. He'd pushed Armstrong over the cliff and now he was trying to convince himself it had been just what the guy needed.

The bell rang. They parted, went to their seats, Bill now thinking of the practice last night.

Some boys at that practice – particularly Alec Mitchell – hadn't tried very hard to cover up their disappointment that this potential championship team had been hurt so badly. Bill had felt it. So he had stayed after the workout. When the others were gone Mr. Turner hoisted himself on the equipment trunk and lighted his pipe. For a while they talked about Fat. The little guy had shown a remarkable amount of fight to retain his accidental position as substitute goalie. Several other boys had come out to try for the job, but none had been any better than Fat. "The trouble is," the coach said, "Fat is terrible. But the others are worse. And I think we've tried every kid in school who's ever played goal. I sure hope we never have to use him. . . ." He puffed on his pipe a few times to get it going again after that speech, then said, "How about you, kid? Is this Armstrong talk-talk-talk getting you down?"

"Some." It was a vast understatement.

"Remember Pete's trouble last year? The crowd was down on him, like they are on you now. Finally he found what we all find, eventually. In any team game, when people get down on a guy, he can't do a thing but give all he's got. Eventually, it's always good enough."

These thoughts were interrupted because class work was starting. Bill opened his algebra book. He had to stick it out. Armstrong had been able to run away from it, make a simple decision to go back to Brandon. Pete hadn't been able to run away. And neither would he, Bill Spunska. If only nothing more happened, if only they could beat Daniel Mac tomorrow night, it shouldn't be so bad . . .

Gordon Bell and St. John's met in the first game the next night. They were tied for third, two points back of Northwest in the standings. A win for either would have jumped the winner over second-place Kelvin into a tie for first with Northwest. But St. John's came back strongly in the third period to tie 5–5, so each advanced only a point. Now there were three clubs only one point behind Northwest.

The crowd heckled Northwest again as they came to the ice, but it didn't take the starch out of Bill as it had last week. This time it was the reverse. He'd come to the ice tonight after a full week of feeling that the whole world was talking behind his back. He showed it in the warm-up, growled back at someone who heckled him from one of the rail seats, and when the referee dropped the puck at centre ice it was as if someone had pushed the plunger on a charge of dynamite. On that very first play the puck came back to Bill and he bulled his way down centre ice, straight down, turning aside for no one, knocked down both Daniel Mac defencemen when they converged on him, and just about tore a hole in the back of the net with his shot. He almost did it again, a few minutes later. For a while he thought the bad weather had been brief, now was gone.

But then the makeshift nature of the Northwest lineup began to show. Daniel's high scorer, Chum Blackburn, was outskating Rosy, who was up on Armstrong's wing position again. In the tenth minute Blackburn tied the score. Bill dashed the length of the ice again and passed to Pincher Martin in front of the nets for another goal, to put Northwest ahead again. But on the next line change Cam McKay, a Daniel Mac defenceman, made a play that ended with a pass on which Blackburn outskated Rosy again and scored to tie it up.

The worst of it was that as the game went on Red saw that the first line wasn't the only one that had failed to come back to full effectiveness. Mitchell wasn't playing his usual steady game at right wing for the Berton line. When Red switched lines once to get Mitchell checking Blackburn, the Daniel Mac speed merchant outplayed Mitch even more than he had Rosy. Finally Red sent Pincher Martin's line out against the best Daniel line, of White, Blackburn and Peters. That seemed to work better, for a while. But covering up for weakness in one or two positions can tire a whole team, and that's what happened to Northwest.

Back on the blueline, it was the second period before Bill began to feel the strain. He rushed less and less. The fire was still there but now he began to save it for the hard work of defence. Not that the weakening could be noticed for a while. For apart from the two lapses that had cost goals – both results of the patchwork lineup – Northwest dominated play by a wide margin. Only great work by Lonny Riel in the Daniel goal held them out, and he couldn't hold out forever.

Midway in the period Pete, playing as if to make up all by himself for the loss of his star winger, shook off his check in front of the Daniel Mac goal, shot, picked up his own rebound, and scored. A minute later he sent Stretch flying around the Daniel defence without a stick or a check being laid on him, and his rising shot beat the Daniel goalie all the way. Now it was 4–2 for Northwest.

It stayed 4–2 into the middle of the third period, when Bill and Gord Jamieson, dead tired, came off for a rest, Grouchy and Warren going on.

"How's it going?" Red asked, from behind the bench. They were leading, sure, but he had seen the strain. He was worried.

"Tough enough," Jamieson said, panting.

"Lot of extra load on you guys back on defence," Red said. "Hope you can hold out."

"We can," Bill said. They had to hold out, that was all.

Red said, "I hope Grouchy can."

Bill looked out now to where Grouchy was crouched, watching a puck carrier, then skating with him, shutting him off into the boards, taking the puck from him, looking for someone in position for a pass. There was no one.

"Stay back!" Red yelled. "Stay back!"

Grouchy rounded the back of the net, head up, looking again for a good play. The centre was open. Grouchy was going to take it up himself. Bill watched him speed up and cross the Northwest blueline, hearing the crowd's rising roar, knowing the decision Grouchy had had to make, flesh against spirit, thinking it would have been forgivable if he'd made any play, any play at all, to save his strength for the hard crushing work of playing defence behind a lame-duck forward line. But Grouchy was past centre, his powerful legs pumping. Yet suddenly there wasn't exactly the same fire to the rush; something almost imperceptible was missing. Bill and everyone on the bench could see Grouchy's tiredness. He failed to split the defence. He fell. He scrambled up again laboriously and dug in with his head down to get back in position for the return rush. Pete was in worrying the puck carrier, giving Grouchy time to get back.

He made it and turned at the blueline, the picture of fatigue, bent nearly double to get his breath back, watching the play. But Red glanced along the bench at his other defence pair, still breathing hard, and decided that Grouchy and Warren had to be good for another half a minute.

He knew they weren't but he had to decide they were. He was playing his strength, saving it, rationing it, giving it in transfusion only when the men on the ice could no longer go on, and he made the decision to leave Grouchy on. It was a decision that haunted him later.

But he couldn't have counted on what happened. Play came back. The Daniel line had been playing hard and were tiring too, and Stretch and Rosy funnelled the attack in on the defence. Warren made the body check. Then Grouchy had the puck again, at the blueline. Stretch and Rosy had gone by, behind him, but Pete was in position for a quick break. Grouchy fed it to him. Then because there was no one else ready he plowed up the ice again to go in with Pete. Pete veered slightly to the left nearing the defence, and Grouchy dug in on his right and crossed the blueline, calling for the pass. Pete passed. It was a little too far ahead of

Grouchy. He took an extra striding jump to try to get it. But Blackburn had got back. He drew even with Grouchy, skating him off, checking him. And Grouchy, near the boards, suddenly pitched forward, off balance, his right arm out to break his fall. As Blackburn got the puck Grouchy hit the boards with a sickening thud and lay twisting on the ice, rolling finally to his back as the whistle blew.

The Northwest bench emptied in an instant, Bill first among them. He got there just as Grouchy managed to sit up. He was supporting his right wrist with his left hand. His right hand hung awkwardly, wrong, and rested on his upraised knee pad.

"Broken, I think," he said, teeth clenched. Then he couldn't help it. He groaned.

Red said, "Help the captain up gently, boys."

It was the first time in Bill's experience that Red had referred to Grouchy as the captain, but he knew why Red had done it now. Grouchy had broken his wrist in a fall that ordinarily never would have hurt him, a fall he'd taken a hundred times before without mishap, a fall that had meant an injury because Grouchy had been simply too tired to fall right.

Bill kneeled and put his arm around Grouchy's waist and slowly hoisted his friend to his feet. Pete took the other side. As the three skated slowly off the ice, and the crowd clapped, and Daniel Mac players skated alongside telling Grouchy they were sorry for his accident, Bill thought: here we are, the three of us who used to meet at the rink at six in the morning so I could learn this game, and Grouchy got this trying to hold up a team shot full of holes by something that was my fault. As they neared the gate leading downstairs he could see hurrying from one of the boxes the young doctor who was in attendance at all the games. Two St. John Ambulance corpsmen met them at the gate and took over the job of supporting Grouchy. Just as he stepped off the ice, he turned and said to Bill and Pete, with an attempt at a grin, "I'll be back for the playoffs. Wouldn't miss playing against Armstrong for the world. . . ."

Bill skated back up the ice to the bench with his eyes not functioning properly. Playoffs. If Northwest could make them now.

Red said, "You and Gord go out there, Bill. Warren will spell each one of you now and again."

The bench was quiet now, stunned. Without another second of play, a lot had gone out of this team just because Grouchy skated off the ice.

They hung on to the 4–2 lead for the next four minutes, pressure gradually growing. Brabant played goal like a magician. Bill, Warren, Jamieson . . . one would leave the ice staggering with fatigue and sit for a minute or two and go back on again. Then it was time to pay the piper. The team had been overworked even before Grouchy was hurt. Now it was worse. Try as they would, they began to fade. Blackie White went from end to end of the rink alone and went around Bill like a meteor and beat Brabant with a blistering shot to cut the margin to 4–3 for Northwest. Then George Peters sped in fast around Jamieson as gangling Chum Blackburn blasted a shot from the blueline. The rebound got away from Brabant. Out it came, as Peters arrived, and he plugged it right back and the score was tied. Two minutes later, in the last minute of play, White and Blackburn and Peters came flying in on a three-man breakaway. Passes went this way and that. Jamieson missed a check. Bill made one but got taken out of the play himself. There was a scramble around Brabant and when the last body fell to the ice the puck was in the net for Daniel Mac's fifth goal, and that's how the game ended: Daniel McIntyre 5, Northwest 4, for Northwest's second straight loss and Daniel Mac's first win of the season.

Bill had played it hard. But one hard game was not enough. The hecklers around the dressing room stairs were on him.

"Hey, Spunska, like to have Armstrong back now?"

"Bet you wished you'd buttoned your lip!"

He knew the hecklers had lessened, but were not yet stilled. He wondered how long it would take.

When the tired, beaten Northwesters got to the dressing room, Grouchy was gone. A rink attendant said, "The doctor said to tell you it was like the boy thought, his wrist is broken. Not too bad a break. One of the small bones, he thinks."

"Not too bad a break!" Red said, disgustedly. "That's a good one."

"The boy left a message, too," the rink attendant said.

"What's that?" Red asked.

"Said Spunska was to be captain until he got back."

The words hung in the quiet dressing room, spoken by a man who didn't know what they meant until he had said them, and then, abashed by the silence they had created, he hurried out and away.

Bill stood in the middle of the floor. Right or wrong, he'd got the team into this mess. Now he was being told he was the guy to lead them out of it – or fail to lead them out of it. He looked around at the faces. Pete. Pincher. Rosy. Red. Fat. All the others. They all looked right back at him as if weighing him. Then he looked at Red again and Red said, "You're it, Bill."

"I'm it," Bill said.

He dropped his eyes and went to the bench along the wall, and for some reason then he was thinking about Mitch. Armstrong was gone. Couldn't get him back. But Mitch, Armstrong's friend, had played a dull and lusterless game tonight. Mitch, this last week, seemed to have been the crystallization of all the resentment felt by others at the school against Bill for causing Armstrong to leave. He wondered how he could get to Mitch, get him back playing the game he could play.

The answer came with the touch of a hand on his shoulder. He looked up. It was Mitch. "I played a lousy game tonight," he said. "Last week, too. A guy can't stay sore forever, especially watching the way you played tonight. I tried to buck up after Grouchy got hurt, but it was too late. I'll do better the next time."

Bill looked around. Pete was grinning at him. Red, too.

"Amen," said Rosy, with great unction. Everybody started talking at once. In some ways the prospect had never been worse, but something had come back to this hockey team.

CHAPTER 13 ▬

The next night, after Bill had polished off a mound of his mother's special cabbage rolls, his favourite meal, he reached into his pocket and brought out his pay envelope. He shook it, looking down into it, and brought out five ten-dollar bills. He stuffed the rest into his pocket. Dad had been quiet tonight. In conversation Mother had been covering up for him. That was a good barometer of the way Dad was feeling. When Mother started talking a lot, it was usually because she hoped that no one then would notice that Dad wasn't talking at all.

"How're we coming with the national debt?" Bill asked, as he handed over his contribution.

"Not so well, son," he said.

"What's the matter?"

He glanced at his wife, and Bill realized that whatever it was, she already knew. "I had a phone call from the night school today. The enrolment in languages has fallen so much that they're going to unite two classes. They won't need me any more." His face at this instant had an almost beaten look. Bill knew that he hadn't liked the job at night school, but it had meant a hundred and fifty dollars extra a week. With that and Bill's help they'd been making good headway.

"How about the mortgage company?" Bill asked. "They won't get too worried, will they, if we slow up a little temporarily?"

Dad got up and left the table and came back with one of the cigars Bill had given him for Christmas. He'd been smoking them one a night since then. They must be almost finished. He lighted the cigar and puffed on it once or twice, but it didn't bring the usual satisfied look. "I'll get something else. Tutoring. Something. Shouldn't be too difficult." But he didn't sound sure at all.

Bill couldn't help a dampening of the spirit, too. Sometimes lately he'd caught himself regretting this work at Desmond's. He fought against it, feeling that it was disloyalty when they had treated him so well, but he couldn't help thinking sometimes as he rushed around in the routine of making up orders that he'd like to be skating this afternoon, or playing chess with Pete, or just sitting around talking or reading. When he had those thoughts he'd put them away.

"I'll get something," Dad said again.

"Don't worry, Andrew," Mother said. "Please don't worry."

He retired with the paper. Bill had a date with Sarah to go to a movie tonight. Now he suddenly regretted that. It seemed wrong for him to be spending on his own amusement. Heck, Mother and Dad hardly ever went out.

Then he thought of something. "Hey, Dad!" he said. "Don't get a job for two weeks anyway and you and Mother can come and see us play Kelvin!"

Because of the night school job, they'd never seen Northwest play. Now they could.

"Maybe we'll win it for you!" he said. "I'd sure like to!"

Mother said, "Andrew, going to a game would be good."

"It would." Dad got up and walked around, and Bill was glad to see the change in his spirits. "You know," Dad went on, "it's a weakness of human nature, this worrying. . . . I don't know why I just thought of it, Bill, when you mentioned the game, but I just remembered that five years ago you'd never seen a hockey game either and I didn't know even where you and your mother were. Then I really had something to worry about!"

Mother was smiling at him, happier now. "This is a small thing, like any worry of money."

Still, Bill was slightly preoccupied that night as he and Sarah went downtown. She noticed it, and there was something resembling his mother's methods in the way she tried to get him to forget it by telling him funny stories about the people who had tried out for Armstrong's part in *Life with Father*.

"We won't put it on January the twenty-sixth, when we'd hoped," she said. "That's one sure thing. We need somebody big, with a big voice. Like you or Armstrong. Say, how about you?"

"I'm still occupied," he said.

"Couldn't you try? Read it at night, do it like that?"

He shook his head. "I couldn't, Sarah."

She kept on arguing, as hard as ever to convince, until perhaps both were reminded of that first argument they'd had about the part. Bill was, anyway. And Sarah stopped in mid-sentence and when they smiled at one another she was somewhat embarrassed.

Sunday Grouchy came over. He was wearing a cast on his right wrist. He was in the depths. Bill tried to steer the conversation away a dozen times, but Grouchy kept coming back to the injury, telling about how he should have fallen, he didn't need to fall, he could have leaned out on Blackburn instead of pitching forward. If he kept this up, Bill could see a difficult three weeks with Grouchy. "You guys just win one, get into the final, that's all," Grouchy said morosely, when he left about one. "In three weeks I'll be able to play."

They were at the door, but Bill held it closed.

"Who says you'll be able to play in three weeks?"

"The doctor."

"I don't believe it!"

"He did say that!"

Grouchy grinned. "He said if I was as big a fool as he thought I was, I'd be able to play in three weeks with a light cast."

Bill laughed. Grouchy apparently had taken the doctor's indictment as nothing more or less than his due – and he'd play anyway. But, let's see. Next week Northwest had no game. In two weeks came the one with Kelvin. Then they'd meet Gordon Bell in the last league game. Unless they beat Kelvin – and Bill was realist enough to know that if they did, it would be a miracle – they'd really have to win against Gordon Bell. And if Grouchy was back, even with a cast, they'd have a better chance, for sure.

He had a sandwich, then went skating. The corner rink, a big rough square of ice rimmed by snowbanks thrown up by the scrapers, was jammed with kids. He practised backward turns for a few dozen circuits and then picked up his stick and got into a pickup hockey game that had been going full blast since early in the day.

People dropped in, dropped out, but the game went on, adults and boys alike playing. Even a few girls. Some men came out every Sunday like this, wearing moth-eaten hockey sweaters, old skates, puffing, blowing, having the time of their life. Some had sons there, too. As in similar games on similar rinks all across the country, the goals were marked by two pieces of snow, tended by the smallest kids. One in this game wore overshoes instead of skates. When the ice got heavy from so many skating, the game abruptly stopped, everyone grabbed a scraper or broom, cleared it quickly, and then the puck was thrown in and away they went again. A couple of hours passed before Bill, gently blocking a fierce little guy of ten or eleven who had body-checked him, decided he'd had enough. He skated to the side of the rink, sat on a plank laid on a snowbank, and swiftly began taking off his skates, his fingers stiff with cold because he had to take off his mitts.

"Can't take it, eh, Spunska?" one of the adults yelled as he went by.

"Too tough a league for me," Bill called back. But he went home feeling good. It was good to play problemless hockey once in a while.

At home he helped demolish a pot roast. Then, with the windows quite black now in the early winter night, he felt too restless to sit still. He had got his homework done earlier, and although he could have found something to study or read if he'd really tried, he didn't feel like trying. Partly he was thinking about Dad, partly about Sarah, partly about Grouchy. He wandered around the rugless floors of the living room and dining room until he strayed into the kitchen by mistake and his mother shoved a dish towel into his hand. When he was finished drying the dishes he said, "I think I'll go over and see Pete and Sarah."

And then, as he said it, he had an idea. For an instant he stood still, then jammed the dish towel on the towel rack and strode out of the kitchen.

"Right now?" his mother called.

"Right now!" he said.

"What's suddenly so important?"

"I'll tell you after. If it works out."

What an idea! Swiftly, he got into his overshoes and new coat, feeling the good feel of it on his shoulders. He never wore it without getting that feeling, even though it was weeks old now, time he was getting used to it. He stopped for a few seconds in the archway between the hall and the living room. His mother, finished with the dishes, had taken up a rug she was braiding. Dad was reading a heavy black book. Bill had looked at the book earlier. It was *The Life and*

Times of William Lyon Mackenzie and the Rebellion of 1837-38 – part of Dad's brushing up on Canadian history.

"Looks like you two are staying in tonight," Bill said.

"I'm behind on this rug," his mother said.

"I am at the beginning of what I suspect will be a very small military action," his father said.

"I'll be home early," Bill said. Then he dashed out.

The temperature that night was near minus twenty, but it was clear and starry and quiet, except for the shouts of the kids still skating on the open-air rink down the street. Bill's feet crunched in quick steps on the frosty snow along the row of narrow, joined houses of which, back there, the Spunska's was one. A few minutes later he trotted up the steps to the wide veranda of the Gordon house. He knocked, and the door opened almost immediately; and when he saw Sarah, he pulled his hat over his eyes and turned up the collar of his coat over his face and said in a deep voice, "I am a famous Hollywood director. Are you the Miss Sarah Gordon who is playing the mother in Northwest High's *Life with Father*?"

She laughed, and in the hall they bantered as he took off his coat and overshoes. Then she led him into the living room.

"Dad and Mother and Pete have gone to

church," she said. "I stayed home to do the dishes."

"Backslider!"

"How about you?"

"I was there this morning." But he was so full of his idea that he wanted to do something startling, like grabbing her hands and jumping up and down with her as if they were kids. Or, rather, little kids.

"You look awfully cheerful," she said.

"I've thought of someone who could be Father in the play!"

They were only a foot or two apart. He grinned down at her startled eyes. "Who?" she demanded.

"Grouchy!"

Her eyes went round, astonished; then became thoughtful; then she grabbed his hands and they did act like little kids. They talked about it. They laughed. As far as they could judge, he should be good. He had an air of power. Plenty of that. They tried to get Grouchy on the phone and ask him over, but he was out. When Pete got home and stopped laughing he thought it was a good idea, too. And finally, at eight-thirty, they got Grouchy on the phone. Pete drove over in the car and got him. The three of them sprung it on him. Grouchy refused at first. They kidded him, goaded him, told him he owed it to his public, who would be deprived of him for three weeks because of this injury. They told him it would give him something to think about besides his wrist. That final argument did it. The instant Grouchy said yes Sarah phoned the teacher directing the play, Miss Robb. Everyone in the Gordon living room could hear Miss Robb's excited voice saying, "Why, he should be wonderful!"

So that was set. Sarah could stop worrying about the falling apart of this play she'd counted on so much. Grouchy was fixed up with something that would make a busy time out of three weeks he had confessed he'd thought would drive him clean crazy. And Bill thought as he walked home alone, if I only had another hundred and fifty dollars for Dad every week and we had a sure place in the playoffs, I wouldn't have a worry in the world.

CHAPTER 14 ◼

The next two weeks were much better for Bill in one way, much worse in another. On the day after the Daniel Mac game a lot of newspaper and broadcast reports had been given to Grouchy's injury, just mentioning in passing that Bill Spunska had been the high Northwest scorer with one goal and two assists. But during the next week Lee Vincent wrote a couple of paragraphs in his column and called Bill "this country's most improved hockey player." He quoted hockey scouts as comparing some of Bill's rushes against Daniel Mac to the way Bobby Orr had looked before he turned professional back in the sixties. Rosy was delighted at this support of his earlier judgement. And Armstrong wasn't around this time to spoil it with the crack about snowshoes.

The news that Grouchy had named Spunska acting captain had silenced most of the lingering criticism of Spunska left in the school. The flow of praise from the news media did the rest. The talk among hockey fans around the city was that it would be worth going to the next high school double-header "just to see this kid Spunska, if nothing else."

One television commentator coined a nickname for him. It was the day after the Friday night double-header in which Northwest had a bye. The man was talking about the odd situation that had developed. Daniel Mac and St. John's had tied 1-1 and Gordon Bell and Kelvin 4-4, and now four teams were tied for first place with seven points each – all but Daniel Mac, which had four.

"I don't ever remember a setup quite so dramatic," the announcer said. "For weeks Northwest had been bogged down at seven points, watching the others creep up. Once the Northwests were cinches and now they're fighting for their lives. It'll be some game next Friday when Bill Spunska, the Polish Pile Driver, leads Northwest to the ice against Kelvin. . . ."

Mother made a face. "Polish Pile Driver!" she said.

But it made Dad smile, and he hadn't been smiling too often lately. His attempts to minimize the worry hadn't lasted. He tried other night schools in the city without success. He had put an advertisement in a newspaper offering his services as a tutor in French, Polish or German. There had been no replies. And he had just received his first salary payment of the new year and found that a new income-tax rate, put into effect at the beginning of the year, took another few dollars from his pay – and the Spunskas operated on such a narrow margin that a few dollars lost seemed like a calamity.

Now there were no more gatherings at the dining room table on Saturday night to watch the dwindling of the arrears in their debts. Bill handed his money to his dad quietly, and that was that. He knew exactly the sum left, anyway. As of January 16, the Spunska family was $1,000 behind. It made Bill's heart sink. Of course, if Dad could get another part-time job, that would be different. But, as he said one night, reporting another day of nothing doing, trying to make a joke of it, "The labour market for Polish professors continues very weak."

Bill needed overshoes. Those he wore were made useless by holes in the soles. His gloves were worn out. There were many other small things needed around the house, he knew. None ever was mentioned. Bill tried that Saturday to give Dad all his pay. Dad only shook his head in a way that meant no argument.

There was only one good thing. Dad was using this leisure for study. He was studying hours every night, history, biography, everything on Canada he could find. After a night with his books he was happy. And even after only two weeks of this extra study he came home one night elated. That day at lunch at the university someone had been trying to recall a date important in early Canadian history. It happened to be something that Bill's Dad had just read. "When I spoke up with the date," he recounted later at dinner, "there was great laughter at a Pole telling Canadians their history! It was very lucky."

That was a good night to be elated, anyway. It was the night of the Kelvin game, the first Bill's parents would see. When Bill had got home from work a few minutes after six, dropped off at his door by Don Fitzpatrick in the truck, he'd found dinner on the table, waiting. They ate quickly. Dad had a couple of sweaters laid out and ready. Mother had on a good tweed suit that she'd had ever since England.

"I was talking to Pete today," Bill said. "They're going to pick us up. Mrs. Gordon has a meeting, or something, and can't come but the others will be here about quarter to seven. That takes some of the rush off, not having to ride the bus."

"Will Sarah be coming?" Mother asked. "We haven't seen her for weeks."

"She's been busy with the play," Bill said. "She'll be with you tonight."

"How is Grouchy going in the play?" Dad asked.

Bill laughed. "She says he's better than Armstrong ever was. He growls with real authority, Grouchy does."

It was an excited carload of people. Sarah and Mrs. Spunska sat in the back with Bill on one side, and they did most of the talking. Mr. Spunska and Pete sat in the front with Mr. Gordon, who was driving.

"We'll have to ask you a lot of silly questions, I'm afraid, Sarah," Mrs. Spunska said as they parked the car and got out at the Arena. "It is nice of you to sit with us, so we will know when to cheer."

Pete said, "Every time Bill gets the puck, or I get the puck, that's the time to cheer. It's really very simple."

They parted in the lobby. Bill and Sarah, who hadn't spoken much on the way down, found themselves together for a few seconds. Sarah looked up at him and smiled, and Bill smiled back. That was all. But sometimes, Bill found, a smile can be worth a thousand words. This was his first game as captain, and Sarah had told him in the smile how much she wanted to see him win it. He went to the dressing room a lot lighter in spirit than he'd been for weeks – and even kidding himself for the reason. Silly, real silly, to let a mere smile affect him that way.

In the hockey practices the team had had between defeat by Daniel Mac and this game with Kelvin, Red had tried Ward, the right winger off the Three Ghosts line – the kids who'd never been in a game this year – with Pete and Stretch. Ward was only fifteen years old, and light, but he'd looked good. He'd scored goals in practice, playing the position with more command than anyone could have hoped for. But now he faced the big test. And he looked nervous.

Grouchy came to the dressing room, his wrist still in the heavy cast, and for the first time since Bill had known him shook off his taciturnity and did some talking in the minutes before a game. If talking had been usual with him before a game, probably no one would have noticed it. But now as he walked around the dressing room in his overcoat Bill caught Pincher Martin's eye and then Pete's and exchanged looks of amazement with them.

Rosy came over and sat beside Bill and Pete and jerked his head at Grouchy. "I didn't know things were this serious," he said.

"Where've you been the last two weeks?"

"With my 'ead in the sand, I guess," Rosy said. "You mean I should stop being cheerful?"

"For gosh sakes, no!" Pete said. "That would be the last straw."

And that night the team felt good. Bill watched the Chief, usually impassive, skate his circuits with a big grin on his face, talking and laughing with Ward, trying to make the kid feel at home. Others seemed cheerful, too. Scotty McIntosh, who hadn't said a word or displayed an emotion all season up to now, even when he scored his first goal, waved his stick at some kids in the Northwest cheering section. In a box seat were Benny Wong's mother and father, and Benny stopped by them for a few seconds to say "Hello," and Bill looked up and smiled at his own parents and then felt good at the warm smiling round faces of the Wongs as their son left and got back into the circuits.

In fact, everything about the Northwest team that night was at a peak that, Bill thought, couldn't have been bettered.

The only trouble was that Kelvin didn't co-operate.

The first rush Bill made he sensed the determination in the Kelvin team. They could go out in front of the league all alone tonight, if they could win – just as Northwest could go out in front all alone, again, if they could win. Kelvin was missing one of its best men tonight. Zubek, the little guy who'd been so hard to stop in the first game, had the flu. That evened it up some. But Northwest was missing both Armstrong and Grouchy, and it was too much. Bill had to shake off checkers all the way down the ice on his first rush, and when he got to the Kelvin blueline no one was uncovered for a pass and he tried to bash through himself and the Kelvin defence knocked him down, good and properly. In the first period Northwest had only a few shots on Shewan in the Kelvin goal, and he handled them all easily. Brabant had more work to do, but he held Kelvin off the score sheet, too. In the second period, picking up momentum, showing the kind of leadership Northwest had got from Grouchy, too, Bill was through three times on Shewan, gave his hardest shot every time, and every time Shewan moved in time to make a sensational save. In the third, Ward made his only real mistake of the game. He strayed off his wing chasing a loose puck. Paulson, the Kelvin centre, jumped at the break. A quick slap pass went to Stimers, and Ward was left behind, and the sudden play caught Rosy and Warren a little out of position on defence. Stimers went between them. He had one of the hardest shots in the league, and he had time to make it. Brabant didn't have a chance, and that was the only goal of the game.

CHAPTER 15 ▬

In the sports department of the Winnipeg *Telegram* a few days later Lee Vincent was playing hearts with a big cop from the Winnipeg Police Athletic Association. Finally he pushed the cards back. "That's the last one, Fearless," he said. "I've got to get some work done."

"What work is more important than playing hearts?" inquired Fearless, who weighed 254 pounds, had a broad Scots accent, and whose real name was MacTaggart.

"You'd be surprised," Lee said. "Go out and catch a criminal. Come back in an hour or so and I'll give you a chance to get your money back."

Fearless lumbered out, grumbling. Lee got up and paced around the office. "Come on, Boswell," he urged himself, "get to work!" Lee seldom called anyone by his right name, if he could avoid it. When he met a referee he said, "Hello, Blind Man." When he met a coach, he said, "Hello, Mastermind." He glanced at some new sports photos in from a feature service, thumbed through some eastern papers and read some sports columns. Finally he sat down at his computer terminal, opened a drawer, and pulled out a clipping. It was the story he'd written for last Saturday's paper on last week's high school hockey.

He leaned over and studied the clipping, running down through the story to the statistics, which read:

Inter-High Hockey

RESULTS

Kelvin 1	Northwest 0
Daniel McIntyre 4	Gordon Bell 3

STANDINGS

TEAM	PLAYED	WON	LOST	TIED	GOALS FOR	GOALS AGAINST	POINTS
Kelvin	7	3	1	3	13	10	9
Northwest	7	3	3	1	21	15	7
Gordon Bell	7	2	2	3	23	21	7
St. John's	7	2	2	3	17	21	7
Daniel Mac	8	2	4	2	16	23	6

He sighed. What a guessing game. He wondered about Northwest's chances. They would have beaten anybody but Kelvin last week, even though they were weakened. Shewan in goal had been marvelous. . . . Northwest could sure thank Daniel Mac for knocking off Gordon Bell. That Daniel team had been hot lately.

He turned back to his terminal and began to tap the keys.

After a couple of paragraphs he picked up the phone at his elbow, dialed a number, and said, "Mastermind? Lee Vincent. What's the doc say about DeGruchy playing tomorrow night?"

He listened for a while, then said, "Okay. Thanks, Red. Just writing my story. Good luck, boy."

He hung up and began again. A few minutes later he was finished, about to check his story, when the phone rang. He picked it up.

"Sports department," he said. "Who? Squib! When did you get in? Sure, I'll answer any questions you can think up. Come on up. . . ."

He hung up and started to check his story on the video screen, reading from the beginning:

One of the oddities of human nature is that people like so much to see bigness take a fall. They like to see the Yanks beaten, they bet long shots at the races, they cheer when some challenger swings from the floor and lands one on the point of a big man's jaw. And that's why, in the local high school league, they got down on Northwest in the first part of this season. Northwest was a popular underdog last year. This year the underdog grew up and started acting too much like the boss of the block for the fans to like it.

Then lightning struck. Everyone closely connected with hockey in the city knew something was wrong on that team, from the beginning. There was arguing in the dressing room and bickering on the ice. When it blew up, there was a momentary bad taste. St. John's beat Northwest – and that was fine with the fans. They came out the next week hoping that Daniel Mac, which hadn't won a game, would upset the big boys, too. They did. But by the time it was over the fans weren't really sure they wanted Northwest to lose. In that game they saw Spunska emerge as a star. And they saw DeGruchy, a good man, badly hurt. By last week when Northwest skated out against Kelvin the crowd was with them again. This was no longer the league bully. These top dogs had lost their swagger. They staggered out on three legs against a team they'd had trouble beating when they were at full strength. They lost again, their third straight defeat.

When they go out tonight again Gordon Bell, after Kelvin plays St. John's in the opener, they're underdogs again.

They've been humbled, folks. Once they were considered a cinch for the league championship. Now they've got to beat Gordon Bell in this last game, snap a three-game losing streak, or they won't even make the playoffs. Tonight they'll have their captain back, playing with a cast on his wrist. According to Red Turner, the old pro who is Northwest's coach, DeGruchy nagged his doctor into breaking off the first cast and putting on a lighter one which leaves his fingers free. At this writing, Turner didn't know what other changes he'd make in his lineup.

176

The way things stand now, there could be a three-way tie for first after these last two games of the schedule. That would be the result if St. John's upsets Kelvin in the first game, to jump to nine points. Then the winner of the Northwest–Gordon Bell encounter would wind up with nine, too. But if form means anything, Kelvin will beat St. John's to clinch first place. Then the winner between Northwest and Gordon Bell will get the other playoff spot.

He finished reading, thought a minute or two longer, then pushed the button which would automatically set the story in print for tomorrow's paper.

In the sports office at Northwest the next morning Red Turner had covered several sheets of paper with possible lineups for tonight's game with Gordon Bell. Occasionally, he got up and paced through his domain, the big airy gymnasium, busy with volleyball now, the dressing rooms, the drying room for team uniforms, the showers. The decisions he made about his lineup for tonight could be his most important since he came to Northwest. Should I drop Jamieson again, leave Ward on Gordon's line, put Rosy back on defence? Should I drop Ward – but the kid looked good last week, just that one mistake – and put Rosy on the forward line again? But would Rosy's lack of speed be fatal against Gordon Bell? They're the fastest team in the league, especially that first line. . . . Back at his desk he worked on some records for inter-class basketball for a while, but had turned back to the hockey lineup when Fat came in.

"Got a spare period," Fat said. "Anything I can do?"

"Rustle me up a good fortune teller."

"Yeah," Fat said. "I wish I could!" There were other visitors after Fat left – a teacher or two, the gym assistant, a couple of boys looking for a volleyball. About eleven there was another tap on the door.

"Come in," Red called. He glanced up as the door opened, then jumped to his feet. "Well, Squib! Where'd you drop from?"

The Toronto scout was muffled up in a big overcoat, his face wearing a big grin. "From the air," he said. "Yesterday. Gotta go out again right after I see your game tonight."

"What's the rush?"

"Gotta go on out to the West Coast and look at a guy we're thinking of making a deal for. Busy?"

"Not a bit. Sit down." Red wondered if there could be anything to this visit that didn't immediately meet the eye.

Squib sat in the office's other chair and looked around at the filing cabinets, the basketballs and volleyballs stacked in a corner, the sports manufacturers' catalogues, the old picture of Red Turner when he was in his heyday as the big man of the Toronto defence. Then he came to the point.

"Red," he said, "I want to ask you some questions about this Spunska kid."

Red looked up quickly. So that was it! He sparred a little. "What do you think of him?"

Squib took out a dog-eared notebook. "I got it right here," he said, thumbing pages. "I saw him in that first Kelvin game, you know. Wasn't really scouting him at all, that time. But couldn't help noticing him. Here it is. . . . 'Green as grass, but some day might be the best of them all.' I've had him in the back of my mind ever since. And then Lee Vincent wrote that story about the kid looking like the best around. Lee doesn't toss that stuff out lightly. Anyway, I thought I'd better have another look, and a talk with you."

Red picked up a pencil, fiddled with it, and looked out the window. "He isn't so green, now," he said. "He still isn't the greatest skater. But he gets there."

"What about this fight with that other kid, Armstrong? Lost you a good boy. Is Spunska the kind of kid other players can't get along with?"

Red shook his head. "He won't be pushed around. But he's no troublemaker. Armstrong tried to push him around and got it back with a lot of interest." He grinned, remembering, and

179

told about the body check Spunska had thrown at Armstrong in that last practice before Christmas. "I never threw a better check myself, Squib," he said. "Armstrong is hard to hit and Spunska knocked him cold, absolutely cold."

Squib was making notes. "Another thing," he said, "him being acting captain . . . Was that just a bit of whimsey, or something, sentimentality after the ride he was taking?"

Red said, "It was because he was the team's natural leader after DeGruchy was hurt. . . . But you know a lot about the kid!"

Squib said, "I spent a couple of hours with Lee Vincent last night. You two aren't letting your enthusiasm run away with you, are you?"

Red laughed. "Probably."

The scout said, "Well, I can make up my own mind on that. But keep this under your hat, will you?"

"Sure."

Squib got up. "Well," he said. "I'll see the kid again a few times. If you win tonight I'll be back to have another look in the city final. Good luck. . . ."

"Thanks."

When Squib left, Red stared again at the piece of paper on which soon he had to produce a final lineup for tonight. But that conversation just ended kept getting in the way. A kid on his way. Red could remember how it felt. And Bill didn't even know it yet. And another thing, if he looked like a bum tonight, maybe he never would know. . . . That's the way sports went.

He began writing down a lineup.

CHAPTER 16 ▬

Bill didn't know that the Toronto scout was at the game that night until halfway through the first period. Gordon Bell was playing a man short because Bevan had got a two-minute penalty for carrying his stick dangerously high. The Northwest power play had been buzzing around Gordon Bell goal without scoring, when suddenly a hard shot by the Chief hit a skate and caromed into the centre zone and Bill and Buck Forsyth, the big Gordon Bell defenceman, were racing after it – and Forsyth had a head start, no one between him and Brabant in Northwest's goal.

At that instant, with the crowd's sudden surprised yell now prolonged, Bill heard none of the crowd noise, only the noise of his breath and his skates and Forsyth's skates. The puck had come to rest along the boards in front of the timer's bench. But Forsyth would have to go in to pick up the puck and then cut out again toward the Northwest goal; and on the fly Bill decided how he would do it, seeing the angle Forsyth would take. If Bill could get to the boards before the big guy went by, he'd have him. He was nearly there as Forsyth had to slow a shade to pick up the puck and Bill crouched and came up as he hit and the impact staggered him, but Forsyth went right over the boards near the players' bench and landed in the lap of a little man sitting at the rail; and in the instant of seeing, as Bill tipped the puck to Hurry Berton – going by on the fly, turning to go back in to the attack again – he saw that it was the man he'd seen earlier in the season with Lee Vincent. The Toronto scout!

And before Forsyth could struggle back to the ice again, the five Northwesters were swarming in around the Gordon Bell defence again; and little Paul Finnigan, the goalie, kicked out three before a rebound went straight out in front and Bill, inside the blueline, saw it coming and met it and shot all in one motion, and as Finnigan dove to stop it the puck hit his stick and knocked it sideways and bounced into the net, and on the bench and on the ice Northwest sticks went into the air for the first goal.

Bill didn't think again about the Toronto scout for a while. On the bench, a minute later, he watched with a wince he couldn't control when Grouchy, cast and all, threw his first body check of the game and knocked down Bevan.

Pincher said, along the bench, "Sure good to have *him* back on defence."

The defence felt good tonight, Rosy and Bill, Grouchy and Warren, the old first-string defence pairs. Red had decided eventually that he couldn't afford to use Rosy as a forward tonight against this lightning-fast Gordon Bell team. Ward, for all his inexperience, could skate like the wind and in the dressing room before the game Red had spent a couple of minutes telling him that his job tonight was to stay on top of Jones. "I don't care if you never even get a shot on goal," Red had said. "Just shadow that Jones kid. Follow him right to the bench."

"If he goes to the bathroom," Rosy had chimed in, "you go too, Ward."

Ward was doing as he'd been told. While he didn't add anything to the scoring power of Pete's line that way, right now out on the ice he was half a step ahead of Jones, head turned to watch Jones rather than the play. And the fact that he had kept the little Gordon Bell speed artist within reach all the time had let Grouchy get settled away in his new role as a purely defensive defenceman. After a few shots in the warm-up before the game, he had confessed to Red that he couldn't get any power out of that right wrist. So Red had told him not to try. He could handle the puck well enough to pass. That was enough. And now, able to concentrate entirely on defence, he was impregnable back there. Bill liked Jamieson, thought he was a good hockey player, but there was no doubt about it, getting Grouchy back had made a great defence out of one that had been good but not great without him.

Nice to get a goal while that scout was watching, Bill suddenly thought. But that isn't the big thing. Forget the scout.

The game wore on through the rest of the first period and deep into the second. That one Northwest goal loomed bigger and bigger.

Then something happened that for a few minutes made every man on the Northwest team go sick inside. Brabant dove into a pile-up to get a loose puck, a man fell on him, another, and another. When they were pulled off, Brabant lay still. The Northwesters gathered round with long faces, Fat down on the ice cushioning Brabant's head. He seemed to be out cold. Fat worked on him for a few seconds and then looked up at the coach and said quietly, "Want me to go in goal, Coach?"

Brabant immediately came to. He was groggy, but he had heard what Fat said. When he was on his feet again he told Bill that when he heard Fat's words it was as if someone had shoved a pound of smelling salts under his nose. In a minute or two he was all right again.

"I have great medicinal qualities," Fat

grumbled dryly, as he headed back for the bench. "I should be a doctor."

Then Scotty McIntosh got his first penalty of the season for an accidental trip. It cost a goal by Bush, on a shot from a scramble after Forsyth had knocked Bill down with a clean check. Later Bevan got another after Brabant had turned aside four hard shots in about ten seconds and couldn't handle the fifth. So the Northwesters came out for the last period one goal down with twenty minutes in which to prove that they belonged in the final with Kelvin.

The pressure built up through the first minutes of the period until the crowd noise was one long roar, and Bill was playing the game of his life. Every time he got the puck and headed up centre ice in that reckless headlong clumsy charge, the crowd came to its feet as if pulled by strings. Forsyth knocked him down. Bill knocked Forsyth down. He hook-checked the puck away from Bush and sent Pete away flying in a rush that wound up in the Gordon Bell goalmouth but Finnigan held it out. With Brabant out of his goal once, Bill went to his knees in front of a shot by Bush and it bounced off his knee guards with a report like a rifle and then he sprang to his feet and led another attack, another, another. . . . And still Gordon Bell hung on to that one-goal lead, and Scotty

McIntosh was almost weeping on the bench, saying over and over that his penalty had put them in the hole, it was his fault.

"We'll get it back!"

From the stands above Mrs. Spunska looked down on her son on the bench and remembered times when he hadn't been a big dark boy with a strained face and eyes following every foot the puck travelled, times when he would have known she was here, as she was sure he'd altogether forgotten now. When Bill was on the ice his dad looked down and saw something in him that was familiar, something that lifted him out of this rink to other times in his life when he had seen men fighting for things more important than a hockey game, men who seemed beaten but didn't admit it and therefore never could be beaten. A few seats above them Sarah had stopped shouting with the others and sat with her hands clenched in her lap and her face pale with the strain of hoping. And along the rail Squib Jackson put away his notebook. There are some things a man can remember without a notebook. He was just wondering when the break would come, because he had been in hockey a long time and, although there were only six minutes left now in the game, he was sure no team could stand the pressure Gordon Bell was getting now.

When the break did come, it was in an inauspicious way. Jones took a pass and at that instant Ward checked him. They both went down. Rosy, dashing at Jones, fell over them. The puck went free and Bill got it, and the whole Gordon Bell team seemed mesmerized by the memory of other solo rushes, and in moving to him they left Pete free for a second. Bill passed. Pete got it. Ward was still down. Bill dashed to Ward's position on right wing as Pete sped in on the Gordon Bell defence, head up, weaving a bit, letting Bill and Stretch get flying past him. His pass went to Stretch because he was sure everyone would look for it to go to Bill. Then he slipped in through the Gordon Bell defence himself and Stretch was crashed into the boards and Pete went into the corner and fought for the puck and as he got it he saw Bill barrelling in from right wing. His pass was right to Bill's stick, and still skating hard, Bill shot. Finnigan got only part of a hand on it. It hit the inside top netting and dropped into the back of the net for the tying goal.

And it seemed that Gordon Bell had put everything into holding that lead. Now, when the lead was gone, they had nothing left. Pincher Martin stick-handled in on the Gordon Bell defence a minute later and passed to Scotty McIntosh, and the youngster who had been near tears because he thought he'd lost this game for his team fought his way to the front of the goal with the puck and then coolly drew Finnigan and tucked it in for the winning goal. In the last minute of play, when the Gordon Bell coach had yanked his goalie and was playing six forwards, Rosy got the puck in the mad scramble inside the Northwest blueline and lofted a long shot down the ice and the puck had just enough drive behind it to skid across the line into the empty net.

Northwest 4, Gordon Bell 2. They were in the playoffs.

In the dressing room, Bill dropped down beside Grouchy and banged him a good one on the knee. "Sure good to have you back, even if you are a grouchy old goat."

Grouchy said, "I'm glad I got back in time."

CHAPTER 17 ■

Red Turner thought about Bill Spunska a lot, in the next week, while the team and the school built up to the final with Kelvin. He hadn't seen Squib Jackson after the Gordon Bell game. But Red had been in hockey long enough to know that if Squib had been inclined toward Spunska before that game, he must be much more interested now. For one thing, until the last few weeks Spunska had been little better than a good dark horse. Probably Squib had been the only scout who had noticed him. But now every scout in the area must be at least considering if they should start beating the drums to draft Spunska – draft him very late, sure, but that's what late drafts were used for: the dark horses.

Each year the 21 NHL clubs spent a lot of time and money assessing amateur hockey players the world over, ranking them, discussing them, finally rating them so that when the annual amateur draft came in June they were as ready as the chances of the draft would let them be. The team that finished last in the previous season got first pick, the second-last team second pick, and so on until usually more than 200 players had been drafted. But after the first few, a lot of luck and shrewd judgement was involved. There were players overlooked for many rounds of the draft who developed into stars. That's where shrewd scouting came in – and Red had an idea that if Squib Jackson was as high on Spunska as he seemed to be, he'd be putting in a strong vote that Spunska should be top dark horse on the Leafs' list. Red knew something of the financial troubles of the Spunskas. He sort of wished that the old system still prevailed, the one used before the universal draft came in the 1960s. Back in those old days Squib could have offered Spunska a bonus any time to sign a tryout form, but now financial dealings wait till after the draft. And Red knew that as welcome as money might be then, the Spunskas sure could use it earlier. Like right now.

He was doodling at his desk with a pencil the day before the playoff with Kelvin when Pete Gordon came in. They talked for a while about Kelvin, how in the two games Northwest and Kelvin had played against each other this year each had scored a total of only two goals.

"We've got to get to that Shewan sooner or later," Pete said. "He's awfully good, though."

Red nodded. "I was hearing somewhere that

paid now," Dad said, in a stubborn tone. Not happy, just stubborn.

Bill couldn't speak. On the way from Europe to Canada, he had had a talk with his father. There, with the night rushing past the aircraft bearing them to the new land, Dad had talked a lot about his hopes, how much he was looking forward to getting back again to the peace of university, the pursuit of learning, the life he loved. And now he had it and had to think of giving it up. . . .

"I don't want to leave the university," Dad said. "But I also wish to support my family. Now I cannot. Even with the money we are getting from Bill, we haven't enough. . . ." He held up a shoe so they could see the hole in the sole. "Four hundred dollars for the house taxes, soon. We have hardly any insurance, should have more. It would be different if I could see that next month, or the month after that, it would change. But I cannot see that. In a year or two Bill will be ready for the university. . . ."

"It will change," Mother said. "In a year or two, it will change. . . . Don't you think it will? And this home, Bill's school, all we have gathered . . ."

"I am thinking of it," Dad said.

"But when will you decide?" Mother asked.

"The job begins in June. The letter said that the company would like to know in a week or so if anyone in our department wants it. They will hold it open until then."

After a few minutes of silence, Dad looked up at Bill and smiled. "Tomorrow," he said, "you'll be eighteen."

"I'm going to spend the morning making the cake," Mother said. "You two can spend the evening eating it."

Bill grinned. "I can't eat much before a game. But if we win it – what a birthday present! I'll eat it all when we get home!"

In the morning there was a small parcel beside Bill's plate. He opened it. It was a fine leather wallet that Dad had had for years but seldom used. "I hope you'll be able to keep it fuller than I have been able to," Dad said.

In the dressing room that night before the city final with Kelvin, Pete sat down beside Grouchy. Grouchy's cast was gone now, the skin of his wrist and lower forearm white and soft looking from weeks of being enclosed. The Northwest team was nearly ready for the ice. Red Turner was giving Ward his instructions. Tonight he was to shadow Stimers as closely as he had shadowed Jones last week. Brabant was sitting in a corner nervously banging a rhythm with his stick on the floor.

"I wonder what the heck's the matter with Bill," Pete said in a low voice to Grouchy.

"I noticed it, too. Maybe just this game."

"It's his birthday today," Pete said. "You'd think he'd be happy. Eighteen. Almost a man."

Grouchy glanced down the dressing room and saw the look of adult worry and preoccupation on Bill's face as he laced his skates. "He's a man now, if you ask me."

There was a knock on the dressing room door. Fat opened it. Red glanced up and saw Squib Jackson standing outside crooking a finger at him. Red went out and closed the door. When he saw the grin on Squib's face he sensed what had happened.

Squib waved a telegram. "Just flew in this afternoon from the West and this was waiting for me at the hotel. He's on our list for the draft. I was holding my breath."

Red knew the Leaf owner's reputation: tough and grouchy.

"The good thing about him," Squib said, as if reading Red's mind, "is that when he makes up his mind, that's it. He can't believe that a kid who couldn't skate two years ago can be a pro prospect now, but he says he'll take my word for it."

Red said, a little tartly. "After all, it isn't quite the first time. . . . I can remember Bill Juzda more than forty years ago – just about the same. Two years of organized hockey, then pro. And old Bucko McDonald. Heck, he went pro straight from lacrosse, of all things, never really played much hockey at all. If a kid's a natural, he can make it."

"Well," Squib said. "We'll know better after tonight."

The Kelvin dressing room door was flung open and the team poured into the passage, heading for the ice.

"See you later," Squib said.

Red opened the dressing room door and yelled, "Come on, you guys! All out! One game between us and Brandon. Let's go!"

First two men out the door after Brabant were Pete and Grouchy. Last man out was Spunska.

CHAPTER 18 ◼

Bill never could remember any part of that warm-up. Others told him after that every shot he took almost tore Brabant loose from his skates, but he couldn't remember. It was only when the last people were filing in to the bench that he saw Squib Jackson settle down beside Lee Vincent in the press box. He looked up in the stands to where his mother and father were sitting and waved his stick at them half-heartedly. If he could only somehow make Dad see that he should hold out for another six months, through the summer, then there'd be no more problem.

In that daze he'd gone through the playing of the national anthem, leaving the ice, and now he was on the bench. The referee was at centre, the teams lined up. Beside him on the bench Rosy was looking at him oddly.

"What happened? You sick?"

"I'm okay," Bill said.

Dunsford dropped the puck. With the released yell of the crowd rolling around the rink,

Pete got the draw from Paulson and slapped the puck over to Stretch on left wing and Northwest was sweeping in on the first attack of the game. But as Stretch crossed the blueline, just as he passed, Mannheim hit him. His pass went wild. Josephson had it, turning, gathering speed behind the defence, dashing up his wing with Stretch alongside him slapping at the puck. The pass came over to Stimers. Warren hit him. Brabant kicked out Josephson's shot. Paulson got the rebound but was wide. Pete tried to get it out of there, but Mannheim stepped into him at the blueline and knocked him down and the puck was still in there. And Bill was watching now, trying to forget the nagging worry. *I've got to snap out of this!*

"Get it out!" Red was yelling, behind the Northwest bench.

Ward tried to carry it out. He was checked. Every time Ward got the puck Bill had to think of Armstrong, that long powerful stride, masterful stickhandling. Brandon was murdering all opposition in the west of the province, and Armstrong was the main reason. *My gift to Brandon Collegiate,* Bill thought. . . . Stretch cut in to centre and was almost out when Josephson swept the puck away and passed into the corner to Stimers, who batted it out in front to Paulson. Grouchy knocked Paulson down. Again the puck went back to the corner, again skidded to the goalmouth, again Brabant batted it away. . . .

On the bench, Bill was shifting this way and that with every check. "Why can't they get it out, my gosh!" he said.

"They're trying," Red said behind him. "Kelvin's hot tonight."

"Fine time for them to get 'ot," Rosy said. "The rats!"

Then, in a pile-up around the goal, the puck was free, three feet in front of the crease, four players struggling toward it; and on the bench Bill held himself tense for the second of suspense until Brabant dove out of his nets and fell on it and the whistle went for a face-off beside the net.

Red was shouting urgently above the uproar in the rink.

"Bill. Rosy. Away you go! Pincher! Your line. And get it out!"

The new Northwest team skated to the ice and on the way Bill passed Grouchy and caught his eyes, and saw the startled look there. That had been a bad shift. They'd been lucky to come out of it alive. Kelvin was changing lines, too.

Bill was in front of the net, Rosy ready to dash to cover Mannheim, who was near the blue-line. Pincher, his thin craggy face taut and grim, stood back from the face-off circle with his stick up, his legs braced wide apart, looking around, and then without a motion that could be seen slid gradually in, stick ready, to where Torrance, the Kelvin centre, was waiting for the face-off.

As Pincher reached the painted circle on the ice where Torrance was waiting, Dunsford dropped the puck. Pincher batted Torrance's stick away and slapped the puck to Wong, then tore himself free from Torrance. Wong's pass flicked dangerously out in front of the net, but Pincher was there. And Bill, behind him, saw the artistry that made Pincher a boy everyone had to consider when they were arguing about the league's top centre. He stepped around Hollinger, held the puck; feinted at a defence-man and then with his quick burst of speed was away down the ice, the Kelvin defence digging in to get back in position. The pass went to Wong on left wing and Wong overskated it and Zubek had it and with his quick stiff-legged strides led the Kelvins back to the attack.

The only part of the Northwest team that really held up during the next fifteen minutes was the defence, and Brabant. Brabant, as in previous games, took Shewan in the Kelvin goal as a personal challenge. If Shewan could be that good, he could, too. Three times he robbed Zubek of what looked like sure goals, in the first minutes. He yelled at the forwards, urging them on, telling them to wake up. The defence was playing at least solidly. Red had been a defence-man himself, and knew that his defence was the best-schooled part of his team. He was glad of it now, for Spunska was doing the right things automatically, despite the fact that his usual spirit was missing.

Pete's line, after that badly outplayed start, was slow to come to life. Ward missed almost every pass that came his way, and once when he had a good chance in front of the Kelvin net he got so overanxious that he missed the puck entirely when he tried to golf it in.

Lee Vincent pointed out Kelvin's wide edge on the play to Squib Jackson. "Kelvin's had twelve shots, Northwest only three," he said.

Squib, beside him, said nothing. He looked a little puzzled, watching Spunska.

And then, with a couple of minutes left in the period, Bill picked up a loose puck and pumped his legs hard to get up speed in the powerful, clumsy rush that was peculiarly his own. Head up, he crossed centre ice, seeing the Chief and Mitch both covered. No one ready for a pass. . . . So he shot it in. Paulson started the return rush. Mitch reached in a long sweepcheck to try to get it back. His stick missed the puck and pulled Paulson's legs from under him. The whistle blew and Bill knew without even looking that Mitch was going to get a penalty.

For seconds Mitch kept his eyes down, skating around as if merely ignoring the referee would wipe out the necessity of going off the ice for two minutes and leaving his team shorthanded. But finally laughter in the crowd made him look up and the referee was standing where the infraction had occurred, pointing at him.

The timer's deep voice then was heard on the public address system, "Mitchell, of Northwest, penalty, two minutes, for tripping."

Red left Bill on, but sent out Grouchy, Pete and Stretch. Not counting the goalies, it would be four men against Kelvin's five. Four men to hold out a team that had been knocking on the door since the first face-off. Bill leaned over to get his breath and the sweat dripped from his forehead to the ice. He knew the team had lacked fire, so far. He knew he had lacked fire. Darn it, it wouldn't help anything to blow this game! And at long last the old excitement surged through him. They weren't going to blow it! He'd worry later. He had all his life to worry.

"We can hold 'em!" he yelled suddenly. It was heard on the bench, in the press box, and it seemed the whole team perked up.

"Sure we can!" Pete yelled back, responding. "Watch out, you bums!" Grouchy growled suddenly at the nearest Kelvins. "We'll not only hold you, we'll score a goal!"

They didn't quite accomplish that. The

Kelvins had the one-man advantage. But Pete got the face-off. He took the puck behind his own goal, and stopped. The Kelvin coach was on his feet yelling at his team to get in there. And with a yell Paulson led them in. Pete laid out a pass and Stretch had it, skating like the wind, through the centre zone, in on the Kelvin goal. But Stimers caught him. Then Pete got the puck again and stick-handled in circles at centre ice, was checked, passed to Stretch, who saw Josephson coming and passed back to Bill, who saw three players coming for him and lofted the puck the length of the ice.

A minute gone. But when Pete tried to get in to pick up the puck in the Kelvin end and rag the puck some more, keep it out of danger, Mannheim hit him down and the puck went to Beattie. Paulson was turning at the blueline, his wings forming up. The pass was perfect. Pete dug in to try to get back. But Bill was back. He hit Paulson, but just after the pass went to Josephson. Grouchy and Josephson tangled in a maze of flying elbows and for a split second Grouchy put his hand to his eye and then got back into the play again, slapping at Stimers, who passed the puck to Paulson. He was in the clear! He set himself for a shot and Pete knocked the puck away. It slid across the goal-mouth to Stimers. Brabant jumped across the goal and batted out Stimers' shot, hit the puck off to the side, and as Bill picked it up and stormed out of the Northwest end, Mitchell got back on the ice.

The cheers at this great defensive effort while the team was shorthanded rolled around the rink like thunder, and Grouchy went to the bench with a shiner from the contact with Josephson's elbow.

"Boy," he grumbled to Red, "I'm going to look good Monday night in the play with this shiner."

Red chuckled. "I knew you when you only worried about hockey!"

"That's all I worry about now! But heck, out there in front of all those people with a shiner . . ."

The Kelvins seemed let down at failing to score when they'd had that advantage in manpower. And it was as if Northwest felt that holding out Kelvin then had been a victory in itself. In the last minute of that period they had three good shots at Shewan in the Kelvin goal. But if the rest of the Kelvins had let down a little, Shewan hadn't. He chewed gum a little faster when the Northwests were near, that was all. He kicked out a hard shot from Bill, a close-in drive by Pete, and Stretch's bullet shot from just inside the blueline.

In the second period Northwest had even more of the play. In the press box, Lee Vincent reported to Squib half through the period that on the game, the shots on goal were now even, twenty each. He watched Shewan more closely now, saw him foil Gordon, DeGruchy, Buchanan, and Spunska again on successive rushes. The Northwesters got up from every miss and drove in again. But they couldn't get the puck past Shewan. At the end of the second period there was still no score.

The Northwest dressing room after the second period was dead quiet. Bill sat with Pete on one side and DeGruchy on the other, and Red went from player to player around the room, patting a shoulder here, stopping to give advice there.

At the end of the ten-minute intermission he said only, "You're outplaying them. That Shewan can't keep you out forever. Keep pounding him. Shoot every time you get close to their goal. All right, let's get 'em this period!"

The goal came in the next to last minute of play, and in the end it seemed inevitable that one or the other of the two goalies had to give way. Kelvin had fought back desperately in this third period until they were holding their own, but the game had opened up until both teams were making end to end rushes that piled up on the two impregnable goaltenders. In one seventy-second ganging attack Shewan stopped four close-in shots. At the other end in less than a minute, Brabant kicked out three. Once on the bench when Bill leaned forward a second and closed his eyes, he found he still could see the image of the boy who was holding them out, crouched, intent on the puck, peering, straining, ready for every shot.

They were in there, pouring it on, tired, dogged, trying, in the eighteenth minute, when Beattie on the Kelvin defence saw a break. He slapped a quick pass out to Zubek in the centre zone, who turned, took the pass on the fly. As Bill dug in to get back, Pete went by him, head down, face strained, every stride an effort, and Bill knew that the same fatigue that had him must have them all now. But it had even Zubek. He couldn't get around Rosy so he shot from fifteen feet out. Brabant stopped it cleanly, and then Pete picked it up and turned inside his own blueline and evaded a check by Zubek, and was away, some of the Kelvins behind him. Bill caught up to him on right wing, in the clear, in perfect position for a pass, and the defence moved over toward him a little and that was the play Pete wanted. He decoyed a pass to Bill, moving the defence farther, and then abruptly shifted to the left and went around the defence and was in alone. Bill saw it in that instant as the Kelvins suddenly swirled away from him, realizing they'd been tricked; and three of them were lunging for Pete, a few feet away, no more, when he shot, took the rebound, shot again – and as Red had said, no man could hold out that cascade of shots forever. The last shot went along the ice, an unspectacular shot entirely, but hard, and it hit the inside of the goal post and was in; and Shewan, who had kept out all the ones that should have scored, had been beaten by one that he himself would have called soft.

Bill got to Pete first. Shewan slowly and methodically was berating himself for a no-good human being for not stopping that last one. Bill hugged Pete. The uproar in the rink wouldn't die down. It was still going full blast all through that last minute when Kelvin threw everything at the Northwest team to try to tie the score. They couldn't.

When the last whistle went, the Northwest players rushed at Brabant, hugged him, congratulated one another. But there was something missing. Nobody knew what it was until Red hopped over the boards, clapping the shoulders of his own team as he walked, slipping a little, down the ice to where Shewan slowly was leaving his net. The Kelvin players, silent around Shewan, fell back when they saw Red coming. Red took the Kelvin goalie's hand and shook it.

Bill felt as if they had been waiting for someone to show them the way out of the vacuum.

The players on the bench piled onto the ice; and they all skated down and shook hands with the boys they had body-checked and scrambled with and sometimes almost hated in the heat of the game, and they all went off the ice together, the winners and the losers alike.

"Now for Brandon!" Grouchy yelled as the dressing room door closed behind him.

Now for Brandon, Bill thought, Brandon with Armstrong. The Brandons were just about certain to win their section. They played their final tomorrow night, against a town called Souris. Wonder if Armstrong still holds a grudge? And I wonder, if Dad takes that job in the North, if I'll ever get into this kind of hockey again?

"Cheer up, Tiger!" Pete said.

"I'm cheerful," said Bill.

"Well, smile then!"

Bill smiled.

In the dressing room corridor a few minutes later when Red Turner came out of the North-west room, the sudden burst of bedlam filled the hall and then was gone again, or almost gone, as the door closed. As Red had thought, Squib was in the referees' room, saw him, came out.

"Change your mind any?" Red asked.

"Not a bit."

"I was wishing the other day that we were back in the time twenty years ago when you could sign a kid to a tryout contract right in the season like this, and give him some kind of a bonus."

Squib looked quizzical. "Why would you wish that?"

"They're new to the country, you know. Struggling financially. Medical bills, among others. The kid is working every night after school and Saturdays to help. At the start tonight I'm pretty sure there was something extra bothering him. I can't think of anything it would be except money troubles at home."

Squib looked thoughtful.

"You got any idea how bad it is? I mean, how much they need?"

"Pete Gordon told me Bill had muttered something about he wanted to clear more than a thousand dollars this summer. No kid needs that for himself."

"Jeez," Squib said. "That's a lot."

CHAPTER 19 ◆

When the first newspapers got to John Desmond, Limited, the following day, Albert happened to be up in the front office, picking up some orders from the phone girls. He scanned a paper while he was waiting for an incoming order. Then he grabbed the invoices and the newspaper and hurried back to the warehouse, banging the half door behind him.

"Hey, kid!" he yelled at Bill, down at the other end. "Did you know that provincial final is Tuesday?"

Bill, his arms full of cigarette cartons, looked up from a shelf and called back, "I thought it was Friday?"

"Moved it to Tuesday!"

Bill finished the order and came up front and had a look at the paper, now spread out on the wrapping table. He had a quick glance at the story on last night's game. Pete's picture was with it, as the only goal scorer. And he saw his own name, down in the story. He didn't read it then. But he did read the story about the game's being moved. It explained that the change had been made because other leagues were ready for playoffs, too, and a traffic jam soon would build up around available ice time. Both schools had agreed to the change.

A little while later Grouchy came in through the back door. His shiner was black and blue and green and yellow. He took a ribbing from the warehouse staff. "Not a chance it'll be okay for the play opening Monday," he told Bill. "We'll just have to put in extra lines saying I ran into a door or something."

"Or Josephson's elbow," Bill said.

"This being the poor man's Spencer Tracy is a great strain," Grouchy said.

On Monday there was something different in Dad's bearing when he came home. And he was late. Bill was already home when Dad came in, banging the snow from his overshoes, hanging up his coat.

"Hope I didn't hold up dinner," he called.

"It's just ready," Mother said.

As he entered the living room he said, "Something happened today."

Bill and his mother simultaneously said, "What?" Bill couldn't read from Dad's manner whether it had been good or bad.

Mother had a dish towel in her hands. She sank into a chair, letting it lie quiet in her lap. "Tell us!" she commanded.

"When the head of our department heard that I was considering this job in the North, he called me in and said that if I would stay there might be a chance of an associate professorship in the fall. With more money."

Mother sprang up, went to him, and hugged him. Bill got up, too, and went close, and Dad put one arm around each of them, but his manner was still undecided.

"I take it you both want me to stay," he said.

There was no need to ask. He had just to look at their faces.

"But," he said, "he called it a chance. Not a definite promise. And if it didn't happen . . ."

"It will happen!" Mother said. "He wouldn't have told you about it, if it wasn't sure."

Dad shook his head. "It isn't really sure until the appointment is made! In the meantime, if we wait, maybe this other job will be gone."

"Let it go!" Bill urged.

But the best they could get from him was that he was going to think about it another few days. When Bill went up to do his homework before the three of them walked over to the school to see the play, his mind was full of it. As he sat there trying to solve an algebra problem, his thoughts progressed from there farther afield, into the background of this whole thing. He knew that parents of his friends often owed money and it was part of their lives – it seldom worried them. He sat at his table and looked at his books. It's because we're new that it worries us. He thought of how sometimes at school his reactions were different from those of others. The others were chance takers, with the assurance of people who are safe, know they can get out of any hole. The uncertain can't be chance takers. And we're still uncertain. We can't get used to the fact that every chance isn't necessarily the last one. If we could only believe that, that here chances will always come, that we only have to pick the best one! Bill had suggested that he ask for a full-time job at Desmond's in the summer. Dad had said definitely "No" – that his summer was going to be his own, whatever else happened. To Bill now the situation seemed more up in the air than ever.

Eventually he finished his homework and dressed in his best. Downstairs he picked up the paper. His eye immediately caught a headline:

ARMSTRONG MAKES MINCEMEAT
OF SOURIS DEFENCE, SCORES 5

He read the story. The game had been played Saturday night between Brandon and Souris for the right to come to Winnipeg to play Northwest tomorrow for the Manitoba school championship. As everyone had expected, Brandon had won, 6–1. The story was full of Armstrong. At Brandon he'd got his wish and was a centre again. And as Bill sat reading it he could see Armstrong, the smooth and effortless skating style, the way he could break like a flash, change pace, fool a defence. . . .

"Ready, everybody?" Mother said, coming downstairs. She wore her best dress. It was funny, but although Bill knew his parents didn't have the money of many other parents who would watch the play tonight, none would look better. Dad had only one good suit, but it had been bought in London and it was very good. Mother had this one good dress. She constantly changed it in small ways, but it kept its basic look of fashionable simplicity – and expense.

"Ready," Bill said.

"In the way my students would say," Dad said, getting up, "you look really neat tonight, Tamara."

"Is that good?" Mother asked.

Both assured her that it was good.

Neither of Bill's parents had been in the school auditorium before, and both were impressed. The stage gave an impression of size, although Sarah had told Bill that it was rather shallow for the amount of furniture and props needed to build the illusion of a well-to-do New York home in the lush style of the 1880s. The auditorium seated 400, and the ushers were setting another row of chairs along the back of the last row of seats when Bill led his parents down to seats in the tenth row. Then, seated, they became part of a general neck-craning as parents finally had a chance to see boys and girls they'd been hearing about this year and last.

Five minutes later, the lights dimmed and Miss Robb came out in front of the curtain rather nervously and said she hoped they'd like the play, and to tell their friends that it would be performed again Wednesday and Friday nights. Then the curtains drew back and there was Sarah, looking pretty and acting slightly addlebrained, telling a new maid how to serve breakfast. Her "sons" came in one by one. The audience warmed up quickly. Then downstairs came Father – Grouchy – in a frock coat and striped trousers and with a mustache and graying hair and lines on his face and that monstrous black eye.

There was a small murmur of amusement in the audience and then one of the sons, in a line certainly not in the original play, asked: "What happened to your eye, Father?"

"Accidentally collided with the elbow of a wooden-headed fool named Josephson," Grouchy said.

"Mr. Josephson is a business acquaintance of your father's," Sarah said. "Now, eat your breakfast."

Some of the people who did not know the play or follow the hockey team probably wondered at this chuckle that went through the audience again at this explaining away of "Father's" more robust pursuits. Then, with only that digression, the play went on.

Walking home along the snowy streets two hours later, Bill thought that nothing could have happened that would have been better for tonight. Instead of stewing all evening, he'd been laughing. His dad and mother had forgotten their problems, too. Sarah had been wonderful, better than anybody. Bill had gone back after the play just for a second or two and told her so. Actually, the play had helped him in many ways before tonight, and he thought of them. It had made Sarah see the light on Armstrong; it had given Grouchy a hoist through weeks that would have been empty and painful otherwise; it had given the Spunska family a good night out together. He joined the conversation again, enjoying the walk in the first mild night after the hard cold of midwinter.

The next morning Bill woke early. There was a second or two when he might have got back to sleep, but then a voice in his mind told him as clearly as if it were a real voice, "This is the day we play Brandon." He thought of other things, too, but put them out of his mind. Today he was going to think only of one thing, beating

Brandon. Tomorrow the rest of life could go on. He bunched his pillow under his head. It was dark outside, but with the first blue hint of dawn in the sky. He began to twitch his feet. It was the only sign of nerves he'd ever known. But always, on a day when something big was going to happen, he couldn't keep his feet still. He threw back the covers and kneeled on the bed and waved his hand in the air until he felt the light, then switched it on and looked at the clock. Seven. Much too early. His thoughts ranged around drowsily. Dad and Mother were always promising each other that next on the improvement list around here was getting wall plugs so they could have proper bed lamps. The old hanging bulbs were good for some things, but not for reading. Money, money, money.

Then into his mind came that headline again:

ARMSTRONG MAKES MINCEMEAT
OF SOURIS DEFENCE, SCORES 5

He sank back on the bed and pulled the covers over him again.

Armstrong makes mincemeat of Spunska, scores 5. He tried switching the words around. *Spunska makes mincement of Armstrong, scores 7.* He grinned. His feet stopped twitching. He reached over to his bookcase, paused reluctantly with his hand on *Mutiny on the Bounty*, which he'd been reading. It really should be algebra. They had it first period to-day. Bill wasn't good in algebra. For some reason, when he came to Canada from England he had been ahead of the others in French, history, English, and Latin, but had been behind in science and mathematics. He dropped his hand from *Bounty* and got out of bed and made it in one long rush to his table in the corner, the cold wooden floor stinging his feet. It'd be good when Mother was finished with that braided rug for his room. . . . Gosh, they couldn't leave this place! Then he was back in bed again, with his algebra.

He opened the book, began to read.

All that his eyes could see was:

ARMSTRONG MAKES MINCEMEAT
OF SPUNSKA, SCORES 5

He approached the school about an hour and a half later, walking briskly. Many others were nearing the school. The weather had turned cold and clear, and the sun glittered on the un-broken snow of front yards. Sidewalk snow was packed hard and made a squeaking noise under his feet. He was adjusting his ear muffs often against the probing frost, when he saw Grouchy come out of a street ahead of him.

"Hey, Father!" he yelled.

Grouchy stopped and waited for Bill to come up. Bill told him again how good he'd been in the play. But they didn't get much more chance to talk. Almost every boy who passed called "Hello," or said something about the play or the hockey game. Bill saw Sarah coming from another direction She was wearing a down coat, high boots, a woollen scarf around her head.

"Here comes Mother," Grouchy said. "Must be terrible for you, having your girl friend tied to an old goat like me. . . ."

The three of them turned in together at the school. Then Sarah gave them both her best smile, and her best was very good, and left. Grouchy turned to kid Bill again. Bill beat him to it. "Say!" he said, "I think she's making a play for you, Grouchy!"

Grouchy was startled right out of his poise. "Aw, for . . ."

"I do!" Bill insisted. "See that smile? The way she came right up when she saw you? And it was really Sarah who got you into the play, you know. I won't stand in your way." He walked down the hall to get a drink, leaving Grouchy, red-faced and indignant, muttering, "Aw, for . . . aw, for gosh sakes, can that stuff, you dough head!"

That was a bad day for the teachers at Northwest. They couldn't quite figure it out. In Room 14 of Grade Ten, Scotty McIntosh was called upon to read a poem by Susan Musgrave. As he stumbled through it the English teacher, Ethel Robinson, a shapely and modern young woman who always included younger Canadian writers in her courses, listened with a face that got more and more puzzled. She considered ticking McIntosh off for a bad performance. He usually read well. So she decided to pass it this time. But she interrupted when he was half through.

"That's enough, McIntosh," she said. "Warren, will you finish?"

Knobby Warren sat in front of McIntosh. He had been sitting with his head on his hands, starting at the front of the room. He didn't even have his Susan Musgrave book open. Miss Robinson was past the stage when she liked to embarrass classroom daydreamers by calling on them suddenly, but now she was aware that she'd startled Warren. He got up, flustered, looked back at McIntosh, looked around furtively to see what books were open, could see none, picked one up at random, and began to read "The Highwayman."

> *The wind was a torrent of darkness among the gusty*
> *   trees,*
> *The moon was a. . . .*

Laughter stopped him.

"I'm sorry," he said miserably. "I wasn't listening."

Miss Robinson suddenly remembered a lot of talk that had been going on in the teachers' lunchroom. Silly of her to forget. Why, she'd been talking about it herself, this game, hockey. Had to talk of it, in self-defence, although she knew little about it, hadn't seen a game since she was a kid, although she had agreed to go to this one tonight.

"Go ahead, Warren," she said. "Perhaps 'The Highwayman' is as good as anything at this point."

So Warren carried on. And as a measure of punishment for his inattention, she let him read it all through.

The class of Room 35 was in the biology lab. Rosy, passing by a small aquarium which held tadpoles, suddenly had an impulse. He had to do something. He felt as if he were going to explode. He held up his cartridge pen and pulled the discharge lever and shot ink into the aquarium. He went on to his seat. It was a full minute or two before Mr. Hawthorne, a fat and bumbling man with ferocious eyebrows, noticed that his tadpoles were coming out of the blue murk at full speed, bumping into the glass wall and disappearing again. "Who put ink in the aquarium?" he bellowed.

And Rosy – who had been coming to this room for classes for two years, and in that time had seen the aquarium a dozen times charged with ink, had heard this angry shout for a culprit a dozen times, and never had been present when a boy had owned up – stood up slowly at his seat. Anything was better than just sitting there with every nerve twanging like a violin string.

"I did," he said, his red cheeks paling a little.

Mr. Hawthorne was so startled at this deviation from his usually fruitless inquisition that he was caught momentarily without anything to say. Finally, weakly, he asked, "Why?"

"I don't know," Rosy said.

Mr. Hawthorne paced up and down the front of the room, absent-mindedly waving a stuffed snake. This was one of the boys from that hockey team. No telling what happened to a normally level boy when he got mixed up in that kind of hysteria. That's what it was. Hysteria. But it would be over tonight. He remembered the ticket in his pocket. Wouldn't do to upset the boy.

"Well," he said, "since you are the first boy in my twenty-three years of teaching experience who ever has owned up to putting ink in the aquarium, Duplessis, I am going to recognize this remarkable appearance of an honest man by asking you only not to do it again. Will you agree to that?"

"Yes, sir," said Rosy.

"Sit down, then."

In Room 41 Sarah Gordon finished her French grammar, then started drawing idly on a piece of scrap paper. She glanced every once in a while down the room to where Bill would work for a minute or two, gradually cease, sit staring, and then jerk himself back to reality and go to work again. Queer how she felt she understood him. That was because, for all the difference in size and everything else, he seemed to her a lot like Pete. She was inclined to judge boys by Pete. That is, she expected a boy to be afflicted by impenetrable moods, singing loudly in the bathroom one morning, going through breakfast scarcely speaking a word the next. She wondered if it were true, what Pete said about the Toronto scout watching Bill. She doodled on until it was time to leave the room with Grouchy and go to the auditorium for a brush-up on a few scenes that hadn't gone well last night.

It was funny, at work. Bill noticed it after an hour or so. All the orders he was getting were small ones – a couple of hundred cigarettes, one box of cigars, pipe cleaners, lighter fluid. Herbie was getting the ones calling for heavy cases.

Albert scanned some orders and tossed another batch of light ones at Bill. Bill looked at them and said, "I'll take some of those big ones, if you want." He thought Albert had been absent-minded in distributing the work un-evenly.

"Oh, no, you won't," Albert said.

"Why not?"

Albert said gruffly, "Because I'm the boss, that's why."

Herbie heard the last of it. He laughed. "We're not going to take any chances," he said. "Look good in the paper, wouldn't it, a story saying that Big Bill Spunska played below form because of a pulled muscle or something from overwork under a pack of slave drivers at John Desmond, Limited."

"That's silly!" Bill said. "That heavy stuff never bothers me."

"Tomorrow," Albert said, "you can lift the heavy ones and Herbie the light ones, to even up. But not now." He banged a hand on his desk. "All right! All right! Let's get moving." As Herbie and Bill walked away to make up orders, Albert called after Bill, "And you'd better win tonight or I'll give you every heavy one for the rest of the winter!"

As he worked, words ran through Bill's mind. Northwest High. Winnipeg city high school champions. That was now. Provincial high school champions. That could be tomorrow. Would it be that way? He heard Pete's voice saying one night, "Sure like to make it, my last year." Grouchy's, "Glad I'm back in time." Red's, away back there before the first game of the season, "I think you've got a chance to give

Northwest its first championship." And a dis-
embodied voice which said briskly:

ARMSTRONG MAKES MINCEMEAT
OF SPUNSKA, SCORES 5

CHAPTER 20 ▬

This game was different. The rink was always tense before a game, but not this tense. Was this what they called playoff fever? There wasn't the noise of most games. There were more adults in the crowd. It was 8:25, five minutes before game time, and the only seats left unfilled were a few in the boxes, and they were disappearing one by one. At the north end of the rink the Brandon band was playing and below and above the music was the tense hum of the playoff crowd.

The tension was building up in Bill, too. Each hour since he left work he had thought, now I'm as keyed up as I can get. And each minute that passed the tension got greater. He had eaten lightly. The warm-up skating was some release. But his own excitement fed on that of others. Voices were high and unnatural.

Skating back from a practice shot, Bill saw Armstrong round the Brandon goal with that long smooth stride. To his surprise, he looked at Armstrong with not much feeling one way or another, except that this was a man he had to stop.

But Armstrong hadn't forgotten. Once when Bill went to the Brandon end to recover an overshot puck he went past Armstrong. The rest of the Brandons looked from him to Armstrong and grinned. Armstrong apparently had been talking.

To his own surprise, Bill grinned right back, picked up the puck, and was heading for his own end when Armstrong called, "There goes the local sieve, you guys!"

And it just increased in Bill the resolve that nobody was going through him tonight.

The cheerleaders went into action. First came the Northwest cheer, and then the names of the team, one by one, spelled out and then shouted:

"B-R-A-B-A-N-T – BRABANT!"
"D-E-G-R-U-C-H-Y – DEGRUCHY!"
"W-A-R-R-E-N – WARREN!"

And so on through the team. When they spelled and yelled his name, Bill kept his head down, feeling in himself the pride his parents would have in the stands. In a way, it was more than his own pride – the feeling that they believed in him so he had to come through. But when he thought of his parents he thought of Dad, the job, the problem.

Brandon followed with its yell. As bright television lights came on – a local station was carrying the game as a sports special – game officials were introduced, Dick Dunsford, referee, and two linesmen from Brandon. The pre-game routine was a blur to Bill: the inspection of nets and goal lights, the anthem played by the Brandon band, and the crowd's shout of release, formalities over.

Bill skated to the bench and sat down between Rosy and Pincher Martin and looked down the bench at Wong and Big Canoe and McIntosh and Berton and Mitchell and then glanced back at Fat and the coach behind the bench. The Toronto scout was in the press box again. On the ice Brabant was crouched in goal, his white face whiter than ever; Grouchy at left defence, his features immobile, waiting; Warren chewing gum furiously on right defence, Pete at centre with Ward moving slightly on right wing and Stretch motionless and ready on left. Armstrong came up to the centre spot, facing Pete. They spoke to one another, a brief cool greeting. Bill knew most of the other Brandon names from the stories he'd read about them. That was Adams on right wing, a chunky boy built like Mitchell; Norman on left wing, heavily built, powerful-looking. The defencemen weren't so big, not so big as Kelvin's. They'd be Mercer and Hoyle. And the tall string bean in goal was Jack Edey.

Pete seldom missed a face-off. But he missed this one. Armstrong got it and passed. Stretch intercepted, got it back to Pete. Armstrong abruptly threw a check and knocked Pete down and had the puck and spun in on the Northwest defence, head up, looking over the situation. But before he got to the blueline Warren was forcing him out toward the boards and Armstrong passed. Brabant stopped a shot. Stretch got the puck and on the way out ran into Armstrong and this time Armstrong went down. But he was up fast, digging in with that amazing speed to get back in the play, back up centre until he had Pete covered as Stretch stickhandled across the blueline, looking for a pass receiver, saw none, shot a quick hard shot through the Brandon defence at the goal. Edey kicked it out to the side.

Bill, up with the others on the bench to see the result of the shot, sat down again wondering if Red had decided to play him against Armstrong as little as possible. He hoped not. He watched Armstrong closely now, watching every move, every shift, every change of pace. Armstrong went around Warren and ran into De-Gruchy and down he went again. Adams beat Stretch to a loose puck and fired on Brabant. The rebound came out to Norman. Another shot. Then Grouchy got it and Pete was speeding out of there looking back for the pass and he got it and Ward and Buchanan were skating to catch up, and the play was into the Brandon end again. Steve Mercer, the burly short boy on the Brandon defence, threw a check at Pete, missed, turned to hustle back, didn't make it in time to prevent Pete's hard shot. Edey kicked it into a corner. Armstrong went in after it. Stretch held him against the boards. Face-off in the Brandon end.

"The Berton line!" Red called. "And defence change!"

The five boys were over the boards in a second. Bill passed Grouchy, coming in.

"How's the wrist?"

"Fine."

Not that Grouchy would admit it if it weren't.

The Brandon coach didn't change his team. Bill wondered if this was strategy, too. Armstrong hadn't been able to make much time against Pete. He'd got through Warren twice but Pete had been sticking right to him. So maybe the Brandon coach figures I'm as easy as Warren, and Hurry Berton won't stick like Pete did. We'll see.

For the face-off beside the Brandon goal Bill and Rosy moved up to the Brandon blueline. Armstrong got it again and instead of passing he skated across the ice toward centre and then suddenly got up speed. Bill, charging back toward his own blueline, glanced over his shoulder, saw Armstrong trying to get by on the outside, cut over that way and poked at the puck. Armstrong just about climbed up his back, but Bill had the puck and passed it quickly across to Mitch. Then he was back on the blueline watching the play go away from him again.

But Brandon's first line was tiring. Over the boards, changing as play went on, came the second line. Red changed lines on the go, too, put a fresh line against this Brandon trio. And now Pincher and Scotty and Benny Wong put on one of the pressure plays they sometimes did so well, pinned the Brandons into their own end. Bill and Rosy, playing up, helped keep the puck in there for nearly a minute before a Brandon forward stick-handled his way out and they fell back to the Northwest defence to break up that play.

In the press box Lee Vincent leaned back to speak to Squib Jackson, behind him. "How about Spunska?" he asked.

"Well, I'll learn something here tonight. That Armstrong is as close to a big-league forward as Spunska is likely to see for a while. I'll be interested to see how he handles him."

"You interested in Armstrong, too?"

"Could be."

Lee settled back to his place again to watch,

as the scout was watching, how Spunska would make out against Armstrong now.

In a minute or two, they saw. Adams was driving up his wing, Stretch trying to catch him. Armstrong, ahead of the play, was loafing, deceptively slow, waiting for Adams to make his move. Bill and Rosy moved backward a little, coasting in, and then the pass flicked over and at that instant Spunska stopped moving backward and as Armstrong took the pass Bill hit him, knocked him down hard. Bill had the puck. He charged down left wing, cut into centre, kept right on going as if he were going to charge through the defence. But Stretch had got away from his check and was out in the clear, and Bill passed and Stretch was in, skating like the wind, cutting in to the front of the goal, shooting, and the red light flashed!

The roof just about lifted off the rink. Bill, turning, waving his hands and stick in the air, saw Armstrong stop at the blueline on his way back into the play. In full flight, he stopped on a dime.

And the timer's voice said, "Goal for Northwest, scored by Buchanan. Assist, Spunska."

On the bench, Fat slipped a towel around Bill's neck and went on to the others. Red came up behind. "Nice goal, Stretch. Good play, Bill."

Music. Round one with Armstrong, and he'd won.

Bill asked, turning his head, "What happened to Armstrong? He didn't get back very fast."

Red smiled, one eye on the play now going on, and said, "Are you kidding?"

"No."

"You hit him pretty hard."

And then Bill began to notice that there were a lot of people in the crowd who hadn't forgotten the feud earlier this season that seemed then to have ruined the Northwest team. Every time he got the puck there were yells of, "Watch out, Spunska! Here comes Armstrong!" And when Armstrong got it, he got the same treatment. And Bill began to find that he was concentrating on Armstrong every second. Even from the bench. Twice in the second period there were face-offs in the Brandon end when Armstrong was on. Both times Bill, watching from the bench, saw that Armstrong carried it out himself, cutting out to centre where there was more room for his stick-handling and tricky skating. There was something in it that nagged Bill a little. He was too excited, too full of other aspects of the game, to think it through. But there was something there. And then Pincher Martin got a tripping penalty, a sweepcheck that took Johnson, the Brandon thirdline centre, off his feet. For two minutes Northwest would be a man short.

Red sent out Bill and Rosy and left Wong and McIntosh on. The Brandon coach sent out his first line, one defenceman, and Pengelly, the second-line centre.

And now there weren't enough people to watch Armstrong.

From the face-off behind the Northwest blue-line Adams got it back to Armstrong. Bill hit him. But he couldn't get his stick on the puck. Norman shot. Brabant batted it away to the side. Pengelly got it. Bill checked him but again the pass came too fast. And as he turned that time, Armstrong, up again, was working his way in from the corner. He shifted around Benny Wong, passed to Pengelly, sped to the front of the net. Bill was blocked by Adams trying to get at him. The pass came back from Pengelly as Rosy hit him. Brabant swatted at it with his stick as it came near his crease. But Armstrong pulled it away, and in the same motion fired a backhand. The red light flashed behind the goal. Brandon goal. Game tied.

Arthur Mutchison, the timekeeper, said on the loud-speaker, "Brandon goal, scored by Armstrong. Assist, Pengelly."

It was in the third period that Bill began to notice a difference in class that made Armstrong stand out above the rest. He wouldn't have believed that anyone could outplay Pete. For two periods now Pete had hung onto Armstrong, but now Pete was tiring and Armstrong occasionally was getting clean breaks. And on the wing, too, Bill had to compare Ward with what it would have been like with Armstrong in that spot. Ward was skating with Norman stride for stride, but he was no threat at all around the goal. Pete's valiant efforts to throttle Armstrong made his own attack less effective, too. Northwest just couldn't seem to get a goal.

Gradually it began to seem to Bill that there were only two players on the ice, Bill Spunska and Cliff Armstrong, and they made rush after rush, checked each other, knocked each other down, and now the people in the crowd who never had known the feud between the two except by hearsay saw it played out in hard clean hockey, neither yielding.

Up in the crowd, Mr. Spunska watched the big second hand tick around the clock hanging above centre ice. "Ten minutes, now," he said. Sarah, sitting next to him, her parents on her other side, looked up later as play wore on. "Eight minutes," she said. Bill glanced up from the blueline after a whistle for an offside and said to Rosy, "Six minutes."

"We don't want to be playing here all night," Rosy said. "Why don't you get a goal?" If regulation time ended with the teams still tied, they would play overtime, until someone got a goal.

"Three minutes," said Grouchy to Bill as they passed on defence change, Bill going to the bench. Armstrong had gone to the Brandon bench. The hand of the clock moved around to two as the puck was held against the boards in the Brandon end. The whistle sounded high and shrill for the face-off.

Red acted quickly. "Bill!" he called. "Go in for Warren. Grouchy stays on. Pincher, you get out there. Take the face-off. Chief, you too. And Pete. We'll get the lines back in order as soon as this face-off is over."

Bill hopped to the ice. He hoped the strategy would work. Five of Northwest's most dangerous scorers would be on for a few seconds when the puck would be in the Brandon end.

Armstrong came over the boards with the first Brandon line. The Brandon coach was putting out his best men, too. Armstrong was talking it up with his linemates, and Bill, watching and listening, was thinking again as he had often before that whatever was the matter with Armstrong it didn't show on the ice. He had played this game with everything he had, cleanly, avoiding silly penalties, and the urge to win now was in every ready line of his body as he waited near the face-off spot for the puck to drop.

Bill took up his position just inside the blue-line, watching the centres slide together, Pincher and Armstrong, and something that had been nagging him suddenly came into focus. He saw in his mind the other times there had been face-offs in that end, remembered the way Armstrong had come out from the boards, carrying the puck out up the middle. It hadn't been a dangerous play before because Armstrong was a fine stick-handler. But it never had been fully anticipated before, as Bill anticipated it now. One of the Brandons kept going offside and the referee was refusing to drop the puck. Finally he got back behind the face-off line where he belonged and as the puck dropped Bill knew what he had to do.

Armstrong beat Pincher on the face-off and whirled and sped out toward centre again, carrying it away from the boards.

Bill took off from the blueline as the puck was dropped, as soon as he could see the pattern of this play was the same as those before. In his mind he practically had the goal scored. As he charged in on Armstrong he was congratulating himself on being smart enough to see this pattern and know it could be broken. He bounced off one startled defenceman and then was almost on Armstrong, almost could see the red light flashing after the shot he would make when he knocked Armstrong down, and he set himself for the check and there was a blur in front of him and he hit empty air. He wheeled and the blur had been a shift and Armstrong was yards away picking up speed and Bill charged in pursuit, and in the next few seconds of that chase he had time to call himself every name he could lay his mind to for underrating the skill that was behind Armstrong's confidence every time he took the puck in front of the net that way.

And he saw Grouchy cut off Armstrong at the blueline as Pincher and the Chief got back, too, and the puck slid into the corner and Bill went after it knowing the feeling of reprieve, knowing that on that play a headline could have been written that said Armstrong had made a monkey of Spunska to score Brandon's winning goal. Bill had almost reached the puck when he was hit from the side and then he and Armstrong were fighting to see who'd get it.

They banged at it, shoved each other into the glass shield, kicked it a foot or two this way or that, hauled, pulled, and the puck went back and forth and they never spoke and their breath came in straining, thudding grunts and Bill knew that this boy in spite of all was the best hockey player he'd ever seen. If we had Armstrong we'd be winning the game. He's the whole Brandon team. If he was with us we'd be five goals up. But he's not with us and I'm the reason for that so there's something I haven't paid off.

That was one second. In the next he checked Armstrong with new ferocity, got him away from the puck for a second, and that second was all he needed. *This one's for Armstrong*. He was out of the corner, across the blueline, pushing the puck in front of him, bulling his way up the ice.

In the last few minutes there had been a dozen rushes, a dozen close shots, a dozen dangerous breaks. But this was another and it was bigger and the crowd came up like a fight crowd at the kill. Bill was brushing off sticks and people, through the centre zone, rallying the team behind him. Armstrong caught him and hit him hard from the side, but Bill held the puck and held his balance and kept on going across the other blueline. The roar of voices cheering him on and voices howling for the Brandons to stop him blended into one high sustained note. And he made it nothing fancy. He saw no good pass to make so he didn't make one. The Brandon defencemen hit him and went down and he was barging on in, fighting to control the puck, when he saw the goal looming up. He shot from just outside the crease and then couldn't stop, fell, crashed, and in the end he and Edey and the puck were all in the back of the Brandon goal untangling themselves from the nets, and the goal light was on, and Bill's teammates were hauling him to his feet gently, no backslapping, a little awed. As they got him up Armstrong went by, head down, shaking it; and, without saying anything that would make a withdrawal of anything past, Bill lifted his stick and tapped Armstrong on the seat of his pants and Armstrong gave him a look of surprise and then the ghost of a joyless grin.

The noise lasted for minutes. In it, as it beat around her, Sarah clenched her lower lip in her teeth to stop it from quivering. Mr. Spunska was apologizing to a man in front he'd been pounding during the rush and the man, now trying to untwist his hat, was saying it was all right, he hadn't noticed. As the timer announced the time of the goal, 19:09, last minute of play, 51 seconds to go, Squib Jackson glanced down at the Northwest bench. His eye caught Red Turner's. Between them passed a look that went back a long way, back to other won games, when a man or a boy refused to be beaten. Lee Vincent was peering at a shattered cigar. He sometimes chewed one, unlit. He found that he'd bitten it in two.

CHAPTER 21 ▬

Bill and Pete left the dressing room together. A few disconsolate people were hanging around outside of the closed door of the Brandon room. The door to the referees' room was open and the room empty. Pete carried his skates one in each hand. Bill had tied his skatelaces together and had slung the skates over a shoulder.

"We're walking like a couple of dead men," Pete said.

"That's just the way I feel," Bill said.

"Dead?"

"Yes."

"Race you!"

So that's how it happened that they plunged into the lobby together, laughing, hauling each other back by their coats, struggling, red-faced, and landed right in the middle of a group of six people. Mr. and Mrs. Gordon. Sarah. Mr. and Mrs. Spunska. and Squib Jackson, his mustache bristling, a smile all over his round face.

Pete looked at the melting looks on the faces of the mothers, and Sarah. "Watch out!" he said to Bill. "These women look as if they want to hug somebody!"

"Just for that, we won't!" Sarah said.

Bill's mother slipped her hand into his and gave it a squeeze. Bill wondered how the Toronto scout happened to be in this group. It must have showed, for suddenly everyone was looking at *him* and Sarah came to him impulsively and did hug him, a really close hug. Then the Gordons, suprisingly, left.

After that, a lot of things happened rapidly. Mr. Jackson asked, "How about some coffee?" They thought he meant here in the rink. He didn't. "There's a place downtown," he said. Then Red hailed them, "Hey, wait for me!" Bill's parents just kept looking from one face to another, wondering if hockey people all acted this way.

They went by taxi to a restaurant that Bill had heard other boys and girls in school talk about. He'd never been there before. It was the place a boy took a girl when the occasion was big, a real blowout. They sat in a quiet corner. They ordered, and while they were waiting, Mr. Jackson talked. Bill kept his eyes on the scout's face but after the first words, the words that said the Toronto Maple Leafs were going to draft him and wanted him to come to their training camp in the fall for a tryout, he heard only parts of the rest. It was like a dream, with odd snatches of words in it: ". . . not often a boy can make the jump all the way at once. . . . Probably what you'll do is come back here and finish school and play junior and make not bad pay while you're doing it. . . . But I'll warn you right now as I do every boy, we're drafting maybe ten players every year and we're happy if we get one real keeper out of the ten. . . ."

"Keeper?" Mr. Spunska asked.

"Somebody who makes the big team."

There was a pause, then Squib took a folded piece of paper from his pocket, smoothed it out, and slid it across the table to Bill.

Bill read it. It said, simply, "Tell the kid that if he's still available at the sixth round we'll draft him, send him to hockey school here to improve his skating, and give him a job around the Gardens for the summer that'll pay him $200 a week until camp opens. And you better be right!"

Bill gaped, read it again, as Squib was saying, "I told the boss you needed a full-time job this summer to help your parents, but that I'd rather have you in a skating program. The only thing is, I don't want anybody else to know that it's the sixth round we're talking about. Some other clubs might take a chance at ninth or tenth, but I don't want anybody to start thinking about you as early as the sixth."

Bill looked at his dad and mother. He didn't

say anything but he hoped to hear the words his father slowly said, "That makes up my mind for me, Bill. We're staying. And thanks, son." His voice shook a little on the last three words.

Then Bill was hungry. Nothing could affect that. He finished a mound of chicken à la king, drank a pot of hot chocolate. The five of them went outside and the scout hailed a taxi. Before anyone could interfere, he had paid the driver for the trip.

Bill held the door open for his mother, then turned and gripped the scout's outstretched hand.

"See you in Toronto, Bill."

"Yes," Bill said. "See you then. And thank you."

Bill got in. He waved to the scout and the coach, standing on the curb, and the taxi pulled away. And he sat there beside his parents listening to them talk, discussing it all over and over again, hardly able to believe that by a game their son played so many of their problems had been solved. When Bill's mother suddenly announced that she was sure she was well enough to go back to work in the autumn, Bill's dad looked at her, smiled, and didn't argue.

They talked to Bill sometimes, too; but his thoughts were in a rink he never had seen. In his head there was a TV screen. He was the big dark kid on defence, and a forward line was breaking in on him and he was watching, waiting for the play, throwing the check that broke it up, picking up the puck, getting up speed along the ice, hearing the crowd noise rising. . . .

Dreams again.

But dreams could come true.

SCRUBS ON SKATES by Scott Young
High school hockey star Pete Gordon finds himself on the
worst team in the league when the board of education
changes the school boundaries. Slowly, however, Pete and
his Northwest High "scrubs" turn themselves into
potential champions . . .
0-7710-9088-9 • $5.99

BOY ON DEFENCE by Scott Young
The exciting sequel to *Scrubs on Skates.* When highly
regarded newcomer Cliff Armstrong joins the Northwest
High hockey team, everyone thinks Northwest is a shoo-
in to win the city championship. But tempers are tested
when Cliff feuds with teammates Pete Gordon and Bill
Spunska . . .
0-7710-9089-7 • $5.99

A BOY AT THE LEAF'S CAMP by Scott Young
High schooler Bill Spunska gets the shock – and the
opportunity – of his life when the Toronto Maple Leafs
invite him to their training camp in Peterborough, Ont.
The bestselling companion to *Boy on Defence* and *Scrubs
on Skates.*
0-7710-9090-0 • $5.99

FROZEN FIRE by James Houston
Young Matthew Morgan and his Inuit "brother," Kayak,
face almost certain death in the forbidding Arctic as they
search for Matthew's missing father, a geologist.
0-7710-4244-2 • $5.99

BLACK DIAMONDS by James Houston
Matt Morgan and Kayak join Matt's father and Charlie,
the helicopter pilot, in a quest to find gold on Baffin
Island. However, when the boys strike oil instead, a
disaster threatens to cost all of them their lives. The
sequel to *Frozen Fire.*
0-7710-4248-5 • $5.99